By the Banks of Cottonwood Creek

Book One of the Prairie Pastor Series

Gayle Larson Schuck

By the Banks of Cottonwood Creek
Book One of the Prairie Pastor Series

ISBN-13: 978-1511451178
ISBN-10: 1511451173

Cover photo by Mike LaLonde

*Heartfelt thanks to: My husband, Larry,
for his encouragement and for
reading everything I've ever written;*

*To Jordis Conrad, my friend, first journalism
teacher and faithful proofreader;*

*And to the early readers of this book who
offered suggestions and inspiration.*

*This book is dedicated to the many country
churches that still offer fellowship and spiritual
nourishment to people across America*

*And to the memory of Jeanie Schaefer
who lived with grace and joy
in spite of debilitating illness.*

Chapter 1

Kelly Jorgenson drove the first 700 miles of his journey to a new life with the windows rolled up and the radio off. Who needed more noise? A cacophony of voices and sounds reverberated in his head as he pushed the speed limit, frantic to find peace. The voices in his head didn't lose volume until he'd crossed the desert and saw mountains looming ahead.

Finally, Kelly lowered the window, letting the hot desert air blow over him. A weight lifted from his shoulders as he saw in the rearview mirror a sunset painted orange, cherry and blueberry cream.

He glanced at the snapshot taped to the dashboard. The photo captured Kelly and Kyle forever laughing together at their 16th birthday party, their white-blonde hair glowing in the light from the camera flash. The photo always brought a smile to his somber heart, and a question. What would Kyle be doing right now?

A couple days earlier he'd pulled his pickup and trailer away from his boyhood home in California. He'd glanced in the rearview mirror at that moment, too. His parents stood outside the house watching him go. Kelly's pale brows creased at the memory. Moving away was an agonizing step for him, but all of the concern seemed to be on his part. He strained to remember a tear, a choked voice, anything that revealed his parents were sorry to see him go. Nothing. Well, at least they weren't taking his move too hard.

As he left the old neighborhood that morning, he'd glanced toward the sliver of ocean visible from the stop sign at the corner. He'd spent a lot of time on that beach growing up, knew it as well as he knew his own room. After studying the scene for a moment, he turned right and cruised east past the local mall and his high school, eventually exiting to the tangled freeways that led to Interstate 10.

On the second day of his trip, as peace settled in his heart, his faith returned, bringing a surge of joy. The future, his future, lay at the end of the road. After speeding through the mountains, he'd hurried past the moonscape of Wyoming and South Dakota, stopping only for gas and convenience store food. As he entered North Dakota at high noon, the barren landscape seemed to shimmer in the heat, like in a movie of the old west.

Now, driving north of Bismarck, the scenery changed again. Millions of yellow flowers waved to him in the breeze and the heavenly scent of clover filled the air.

Although he'd only been to North Dakota twice in his life, a strange sense of coming home had begun when he crossed the state line. As he drove, that peculiar sense strengthened. Odd, he thought, California has always been home. Now its importance seemed to recede like the scenes he'd passed on the trip.

When he arrived at the tiny town of Cottonwood City, he noted the gas station, grocery store, bank and café. No fast food places, he thought, no sidewalk cafes, no ocean view. No Kyle. Weary, yet exhilarated, he sped up when he reached the other side of the tiny town. His new home and new life were only five miles away! He followed a narrow highway. Not too many winding roads in this country, he thought. He slowed at an intersection and turned east at a right angle. Maybe that is part of the slower life up here, Kelly thought. You have to slow down once in order to turn in the right direction.

It was late afternoon, but the sun was still high in

the sky when he came over a rise and saw Cottonwood Church gleaming white against the vividly green grass. As he slowed the dusty blue pickup and rental trailer to turn into the church yard, he was shocked to see over a dozen cars and pickups parked there. Why are so many people at the church on a weekday? He stopped and turned off the ignition.

A large banner over the church door read, "Welcome Pastor Kelly!" People rushed over to greet him. He wasn't sure if it was because he was tired or happy, but a lump sprang up in his throat. All the hard work, studying, doubts and fears as he prepared to be a pastor seemed worth it in this one moment. No one had said a word to him yet, but he'd never felt more welcome anywhere. He'd never forget this date. June 11, 2001, the day his new life was really beginning.

The pickup door flew open and Maury Jackson and Tiny Winger dragged him out. They slapped him on the back and took turns giving him "farmer hugs." They didn't seem to notice his watery eyes.

People milled around, waiting for a chance to greet him. Bonnie. Mavis. George. Ken. He suddenly realized he needed to remember all those names!

Then they walked him around back of the church. Big, century-old cottonwood trees shaded the church yard and brought cool relief from the intense sun. Beyond the church yard to the south, a wire fence outlined a small cemetery. Kelly could see the neat rows of wrought iron crosses and marble headstones, some with huge pink flowers blooming near them.

To the west, the land sloped down to Cottonwood Creek, which flowed between the church and the parsonage. Just beyond the church, the creek spread out to form a pool. Some boys were fishing there. Other children chased each other through a nearby pasture in a game of tag. The little creek babbled happily under the footbridge that led to the other side. The parsonage, his new home, sat near a stand of blooming lilacs. Warmth seemed to spread through Kelly's soul. Maybe this is how home is supposed to feel, he thought. Again he found himself struggling to keep his emotions in check, a problem he'd had since Kyle died. He took a deep breath and let it out slowly.

A line of picnic tables covered with red-checked table-cloths completed the storybook scene in the church yard. Women mixed lemonade in gallon jugs and deep-fat fryers sizzled with something that smelled wonderful.

"You came at the right time of year, Pastor," said Maury Jackson, as he tipped back his tall, almost-white cowboy hat. Kelly noticed the toe of one boot tapped the grass as he spoke. "The crops are all planted, but it's too early to begin haying. We took the day off and came out here. We put a fresh coat of paint on some of the walls in your house and the ladies scrubbed everything up. Then they began cooking. We thought we'd all eat together and then help you move in!"

Everyone looked at him, their faces smiling expectantly. He suddenly realized that he was more than a guest. These people were giving him the respect due a new pastor. And they thought he should say something! He felt like a baby bird on its first flight.

"Well. Well. I'm in shock," Kelly stuttered. "I expected to sneak in here and have a peanut butter sandwich before unpacking. I never dreamed you'd all be here."

"Welcome to Cottonwood Creek," someone called out. At that, everyone laughed.

"I don't think anyone has ever felt as welcome as I do at this moment," Kelly said, aware that water threatened to spill from his eyes. "Thank you for your warm hospitality."

"Pastor, would you mind saying the blessing?" Maury

asked. "Then the ladies will serve up some real North Dakota food."

"Ah, yes! Of course!" Kelly stuttered again. He paused for a moment to collect his thoughts. Around him, men closed their eyes and folded their hands. A couple of women shushed their children, who skidded to a stop near the laden tables.

"Lord, thank you for a safe trip and for this place that I know you love very much. Thank you for each person here and for the food that's been provided. And Father, I especially thank you that you are a God of new beginnings. In Jesus' name, amen."

The crowd murmured some amens and then Bonnie Jackson began giving orders. "Pastor, the line starts here, and you will be first in line. Kids, go through the line with your parents." The volume level was going up and Bonnie began to shout to be heard over the crowd. "And no one gets seconds until everyone has their first serving!"

Tiny took off his cap, a grimy, green thing with "Your Friendly Co-op" written on the front. He stuck it in his back pocket and nudged Kelly toward the food-laden tables.

"This looks really good," Kelly said as one of the women dropped something on his plate. The last bag of peanuts he'd purchased at a convenience store hadn't done much to hold off his hunger. He looked closely at his plate and then nodded at Tiny. "What is this?"

"That's fleish kueckla," whispered Tiny.

"Flesh what?"

Tiny nudged him forward again and his plate filled up with potato salad, home-grown radishes and green onions, coleslaw, gelatin salads and homemade buns.

Since everyone else was still in line when they sat down, Kelly looked at Tiny and whispered, "Tell me what this is. Flesh what?"

"Fleish kueckla is a German dish," answered Tiny,

as he chewed down his first bite. "It's a hamburger mix wrapped in homemade dough and deep fried."

"I've never heard of it."

"It's a local dish, made by the Germans from Russia. Taste it, it's real good."

Kelly bit into the crispy crust. He liked it so much that he had a second helping. Then he devoured everything else on his plate. He didn't see the pies until after he'd polished off a great deal of food.

"Strawberry pie? Made with strawberries I just picked this morning," one of the women said.

"Sure. Better make it small, I'm pretty full."

She plopped down a huge piece of pie that oozed strawberries from under a whipped cream hat. As she left, another woman came up to him.

"Oh," she said. "I see you like pie. You'll love my rhubarb cream pie." She set a piece in front of him, right next to the strawberry pie, smiled sweetly and left.

"Tiny, I may need some help here," Kelly said, after studying the situation. There was enough dessert in front of him to last a week.

"Nope," said Tiny, his head down as he shoveled in some macaroni salad. "You have to eat everything. If you don't, they'll remember you forever. If you eat one piece and not the other, one of the women will be crushed. You gotta eat it all," Tiny solemnly advised, his own mouth full.

"I can see the headlines," Kelly moaned. "New pastor explodes at church potluck."

While they ate, a steady stream of new friends stopped by their table and the same conversation recycled over and over.

"I know you're from California, but what town are you from?"

"Redondo Beach."

"Oh, I thought you were from Los Angeles. Never understood why anyone would live there." Almost everyone asked if he thought he could handle a North Dakota winter. Next they asked whether he got his tan at the beach. Other people asked if he knew their brother, cousin or friend who lived in Los Angeles. Many of the older women mentioned he should meet their daughters, nieces, or friends' daughters.

Finally the line of people dwindled. By the time the clean-up committee began putting away the leftovers, Kelly felt fortified to finish moving into his new home. He maneuvered his rig over to the parsonage. Many of the people walked across the Cottonwood Creek footbridge and met him.

"First, I need to walk through the house before we unload everything," Kelly said when he'd climbed out of the pickup. "Last time I was here, I wasn't thinking about furniture." With that, they all laughed and began conversing among themselves.

About that time Mavis Jackson came swinging over the bridge and took him by the arm. "You know, I have kids about your age. I always pray someone will give them a mother's helping hand. And you know what? Someone always does. Anyway, now it's my turn. I'll help you figure out where everything goes."

Kelly smiled at her and squeezed her hand. "Thanks, I could use a mom right now," he said with some relief, thinking of his own mother, now 2,000 miles away. He was smiling, but his heart froze for just a moment. He remembered her funny little smile as he drove away a few days ago. Is Mom okay? he asked himself, before shaking off the dark moment and coming back to the present.

Mavis stood before him expectantly. He nodded at her and said, "This is a little different than the men's dorm at college."

"Hey, you guys," she shouted. "Start unloading while

we go through the house. We'll find some good spots for the furniture." The men seemed to pay attention to her, because as Mavis and Kelly walked through the backdoor, they began opening the trailer.

The craftsman-style house had been built in the 1920s, Mavis explained. It was long and narrow, with a second story. The back door led up some steps into a small utility room that held a washer, dryer, and doors to the basement and garage.

Kelly whistled. "Was this washer and dryer here before?" he asked. When Mavis shook her head no, he said, "I didn't think so. I'm going to appreciate them after sticking quarters in machines for several years."

"That's what we thought," said Mavis. "These are used, but I think they're in good shape. The water heater, water softener and furnace are in the basement. Maury can give you some basic information on them. You'll really appreciate the water softener. We don't have very good water out here. Hard on clothes and pipes and everything else."

The kitchen had a fresh coat of white paint and the flooring was black and white checked tile. The original white painted cupboards stood alongside an aged avocado-colored stove and refrigerator. On one side of the room was a breakfast nook. The downstairs bathroom was just off the kitchen. The windows over the sink and nook both had red checked curtains.

"Someone here likes checks," said Kelly.

"My sister-in-law, Bonnie Jackson," said Mavis. "She loves checks. See here? We stocked the 'fridge and cupboards for you," she said, holding open the refrigerator door.

"Wow, you thought of everything!" said Kelly as he peered in at the milk, fruit, yogurt, eggs and lunch meat. "Thanks!"

"You'll probably get some leftovers from the picnic,

too," Mavis said, eyeing him. When his face brightened at the idea, she gave a knowing smile. Kelly suspected he'd be getting a lot of leftovers in the future.

"And you'll probably need a microwave. We couldn't scare one up," she said as she moved into the dining room.

"Got one," said Kelly. "Hey, I like these rooms," he said standing between the dining and living room. The rooms featured dark mahogany woodwork. The dining room included a built-in hutch, an antique light fixture and the staircase to the second floor.

The living room filled the width of the house and had a red brick fireplace on one end, flanked by built-in bookcases. Wooden pocket doors separated the two rooms. Even the sand color of the somewhat shabby wallpaper seemed just right. Both rooms had hardwood floors covered by braided rugs.

A leaded-glass door opened to a three-season sunroom, which Mavis called a porch. Kelly opened the door and stepped out. White paint covered the floor and wainscot walls. Windows all the way around gave a view of Cottonwood Creek as it wound its way from town. A white wicker love seat, chairs and a table were in the porch. While the room was presently very hot from the summer sun, he could imagine how comfortable it would be when the weather cooled.

Kelly realized he'd been silent quite a while. "Most of my furniture was my grandmother's and it's older than me, but it'll look pretty good in this place," he said.

Upstairs, the master bedroom took up the width of the house over the living room and even had a fireplace on one end. The other end of the hallway opened to a room large enough for a guest bedroom. Another smaller room could serve as a storage space. The large bathroom held a deep tub with legs and the sink with a pink floral skirt.

"Well, what do you think?" asked Mavis.

"Think? Oh, do I like it? You bet I do. This is going to be great," said Kelly, although he took a second look at the floral skirt around the sink.

On the way downstairs, Kelly told Mavis he would use the east end of the living room for his office space. Other than that, he hoped she'd take charge of arranging the furniture.

The men moved the furniture into place in less than an hour. They stored boxes in the rooms where Kelly could unpack them later, while Mavis helped with kitchen boxes. Soon, the last vehicle left the parking area and Kelly was alone in his new home.

He walked slowly through the house. He couldn't believe how at-home his grandmother's table and chairs looked in the dining room. In the living room, her green paisley couch and green wing back chairs surrounded the fireplace. His little television was perched on an end table for now. His desk and chair looked fine across the room next to his book cases and file cabinet. He'd have to unbox and hook up his computer later. Upstairs, the guest room remained unfurnished. His grandmother's bedroom set looked like it belonged in the master bedroom. Although it dated back to the 1960s, Kelly had to admit the soft lines of a French country bureau, dresser, bed and night stands had class. He also had a heavy old rocker that his mother's father had brought to California from North Dakota many years before. It sat by the triple windows looking like it was back home. The ladies had dug bedding out of the old hope chest and made the bed.

Kelly opened one of the windows. The sun hovered in the western sky like a yellow hot air balloon drifting through the air. Some birds called out in the still night air. He went downstairs and outside, hearing for the first time the squeak and slam of the screen door. The wide verandah on the east side of the house held an inviting porch swing. From its seat he could view the picturesque creek, foot bridge and church.

He realized that he hadn't even been inside the church—his church—today. Tomorrow he'd reacquaint himself with the building, but for now he needed to call his parents and Brianna to let them know he made it okay.

That was when he heard a rustling sound in the grass. His heart raced as it often did when he was startled. Would he never get over the feeling of terror that some-times grabbed him? He studied the grass where the sound continued. Was it a rattlesnake? He'd been warned by his friends in California to watch out for them.

Then a furry gray face appeared.

"Meow."

"Oh, hello, kitty," Kelly said with relief. He reached out a hand that shook just a bit and took a deep, calming breath. He tried to pet the cat, but it flattened its ears and pulled back. Its gray fur was matted and rough.

"Hey, it's okay. You want something to eat?" Kelly opened the screen door and bounded up the steps. He brought out a slice of cheese. "Are you hungry?"

The cat stayed as far away as it could from Kelly and still grab the cheese from him. It ate it quickly and looked up at him.

"More? You want more? What's the matter—poor mouse-hunting these days?"

He went back in and brought out a bowl of milk and some sandwich meat, which the cat attacked ravenously. When it had finished, it licked its paws and rubbed up against Kelly as it started to purr.

"Hey you really were hungry," he said, trying to pet the cat again, successfully this time. He wasn't sure he wanted to touch the filthy fur, but his desire to comfort her won out over his disgust. "Do you have a name? You seem awfully thin," he said, feeling the sharp bones in her back.

"Hey, how come you are so thin up here, but you have such a big belly?" he asked. "Oh-oh. Are you in a family way? Where are your home and husband, Madam?"

She climbed up on his lap, purring contentedly. He began to stroke her fur, though he found it a bit repulsive to touch the matted mess. Probably how God feels about being nice to us sometimes, Kelly thought.

"I know your type, I'm afraid. Madam, you are the love 'em and leave 'em type, aren't you?"

"Meooow."

"Oh, you aren't that type? I'm sorry. I didn't mean to insult you. Madam, if you want to spend the night here, it's quite all right."

Kelly got up and the cat followed him around to the garage door. He went in and padded a packing box with some rags.

"Madam, this is the only room we have available at the inn tonight. It's yours if you want it and I think you'll find the rent reasonable." The cat jumped into the box and sat staring at him as though he were invading her private suite. "Okay, Madam, I can take a hint," Kelly said. He left the side door open in case she wanted to leave.

Kelly wandered through the house, bored with the idea of unpacking. He wanted to become more familiar with his new home. The last few years while he was in college he had moved several times, but each apartment or dorm room served only as a temporary place to sleep and study. Now, he realized, this would be his home for the foreseeable future. He'd been too busy with classes and ministry opportunities to miss having a real home, but now it felt good to think about settling in.

He called his parents and tried to reach Brianna before he walked out to the three-season porch and sat down. The sun hung near the horizon now, like an orange ball of fire in the west.

"Lord, you are really good at impressing me with your creativity," he prayed out loud. Reality hit him again. After years of preparation, he was now about to begin doing the work God had called him to do. He remembered the bright faces of the people who had greeted his arrival earlier. Could he live up to their expectations? What about God's expectations? He ran his fingers through his wavy blonde hair, a smile spreading across his face. He would do his best!

Kelly stood and walked around the porch and practiced his new role. "Yes, I'm Pastor Jorgenson. May I help you?" he said in his best pulpit voice. "Yes, I pastor two churches in North Dakota." The smile lingered. This was it! After all the heartache, soul searching and studying, here he was in his own parsonage!

He thought of his classmates at the small seminary from which he'd just graduated. Most were accepting jobs as music ministers or youth pastors on the West Coast. They teased Kelly plenty for accepting a position in North Dakota. They called him Moses and teased him about his journey to the desert. Kelly teased back that he was going to the Promised Land. Still, he had said little to them about his upcoming job. If they knew his parsonage was miles from the nearest town, well, they'd get plenty of mileage out of that, too, he thought with a wince. Only his mentor and pastor, Wallace McDougal, knew the whole story and encouraged his assignment.

At 23, Kelly longed for solitude and hoped his new job might provide plenty of space for thinking and praying and healing. He hoped to fit into the new community. Of Norwegian descent, with fair skin and sand-colored hair, he could see he already looked like a "local." It would definitely be a change from the neighborhood where he grew up where he and Kyle stood out like a pair of sugar cookies.

Memories flooded him as he sank into one of the

wicker chairs, kicked his tennis shoes off and stretched his legs out. His first trip to North Dakota had been for a summer as a counselor at a camp on Lake Metigoshe in the Turtle Mountains on the Canadian border. The camp's clear water and surrounding forest exhilarated Kelly, but not as much as the sense of God's presence that filled the campground and especially the chapel.

He'd had a stronger spiritual encounter than ever before at the remote camp. It seemed as though God spoke to him in every song, sermon, and comment made by campers and counselors. He came to recognize God was speaking to him by the way some words seemed to resonate in his heart, echoing to the very core of his soul. He read his Bible with a renewed appetite for God's word, his ultimate guide for facing life. At the end of the second month, Kelly felt sure he wanted to return to North Dakota.

Even now, four years later, he felt his spirit bubbling inside him as he remembered those exciting days. Whatever was ahead of him in life, at least he could be confident of his call. It amazed him that sometimes things didn't look like he expected them to. When he'd received the call to become a pastor and go to North Dakota so long ago, he pictured himself at the Bible camp again. But here he was a pastor and in North Dakota, but a couple hundred miles from Lake Metigoshe. Oh well, he thought, I'm close enough to visit once in a while.

Memories of camp reminded him of Jim Barnes, the man responsible for his first trip to North Dakota.

"Jim Barnes," Kelly said out loud. "You had no idea what you were starting." Jim lived in North Dakota, but had served in Viet Nam with Kelly's father, Steve Jorgenson. Jim had visited the Jorgenson family at the time when Kelly was deciding his next step. When Jim heard Kelly was looking for a summer job away from the city, he suggested the Metigoshe camp. Jim said his son, Danny, had worked there and really enjoyed it.

"Danny's real religious," Jim had said. "He thought the camp up there was the best thing since toasted marshmallows. Maybe you'd like it, too. In fact, he just got a letter from them asking him to work there again. I'll forward it to you. Danny graduated from college and has some high-powered job out in Chicago, so he won't be working at summer camps anymore."

A couple weeks later the letter arrived. After reading it carefully, Kelly realized that the camp offered everything he wanted: time away from California, someplace remote, working with teens, an opportunity to teach, and private time for reflection. Later he realized the irony of the last item, as he put in 16-20 hour days, but everything else turned out perfect.

When he returned to Los Angeles after that summer, he told his parents he wanted to become a pastor and move to North Dakota. Their smiles had frozen on their faces.

"Sweetie, that sounds very nice, but you have a lot of options. You'll probably want to do a lot of different things before you graduate," his mother, Nancy, had said.

"North Dakota is a long way from home," she continued. "And it gets so cold there. Remember all those stories Grandma used to tell about it being so cold your tongue would freeze to metal? Or how the snow was piled 10 feet high?"

"You're nuts," was his father's only comment. Neither of his parents shared his faith. They occasionally attended church, but even the worst tragedy of their lives, the one that drove Kelly to his knees, had not awakened them spiritually. They seemed to possess just enough inner resources to get them through "without any help from the Almighty," as his father put it.

They didn't understand why he wanted to be a pastor. And, they reasoned his idea of returning to North Dakota would fade. Kelly tried talking to them about his growing faith in God. He'd given them Bibles and books to read. Nothing seemed to open their eyes to the spiritual world around them.

A few years later when Kelly announced he was being considered for a job as a pastor in North Dakota, they seemed surprised, as though they hadn't given the idea another thought. Telling them was hard, because he realized with Kyle gone, it would be more difficult for them to have him move so far away. Wouldn't it?

That's why it was strange a few days ago when his mother's goodbye was as casual as if he were leaving for a trip to the store. Kelly paused in his thoughts. His mother's remoteness had begun to trouble him. Was there something wrong with her?

Of course, there was something wrong, he thought. Suddenly, his worst memories were unlocked: memories of the night his twin brother died.

"Why is it," he moaned in the gloomy silence that seemed to overpower him, "that the most bitter and most sweet are so tangled together? Why does the person you're closest to cause the most pain? Or why is it the biggest tragedy is only a breath away from great victory?"

Kelly knew without a doubt it was Kyle's unexpected death that led him on a search for the meaning of life, a search that ended in his greatest joy and fulfillment.

Kyle died in a shooting shortly before their high school graduation. Kelly, Kyle and Brianna "Bri" Davis, Kyle's girlfriend, had been together when a drunken classmate had accidentally fired a gun. The shot hit and instantly killed Kyle. After the death of his twin, Kelly's life stopped and hung suspended for months. He'd wake almost every night, sweat soaked, certain he'd just heard the gun explode again. He'd taken up drinking and lost himself in alcohol for weeks at a time, trying not to think about Kyle. Then he'd sober up and visit with his brother's pastor, Pastor McDougal as often as possible. He read the Bible, but couldn't make any sense of it.

Unlike Kyle, he'd rarely been in a church and knew little about Christianity. In those weeks after Kyle died, he learned Kyle's faith had been very important to him. Kyle's walk with God began when he attended a Christian concert. Before that time he'd explored a lot of spiritual avenues. There were a lot of alternatives to explore in Southern California. Kelly watched his brother try out a lot of belief systems, but after a few weeks they always lost their appeal.

Once when Kelly asked Kyle why he no longer seemed interested in a particular spiritual view, Kyle shook his head and said, "Like the other things I've tried, it had some truth, but it wasn't the real thing. I want to believe I'm here for a reason and there is solid truth somewhere. I'm going to keep looking until I find it."

After that Christian concert, Kelly actually witnessed Kyle's transformation. First Kyle had been cautious. He'd talked to some friends he knew to be followers of Christ. He spent hours reading a Bible someone gave him. In the following days, Kelly began to see a new light in Kyle's eyes. When he questioned his brother about it, Kyle said, "It's not about being spiritual or religious. That's the good news! It's about a relationship with Jesus. He's alive, Kelly! He didn't just live 2,000 years ago. He's alive and we can talk with him."

Kelly smiled and shrugged, not quite sure what to say.

"It's like this, Kelly, other religions have a lot of requirements to earn salvation. But with Christianity, God gives salvation as a gift. All we need to do is accept His gift. This is real."

As far as Kelly was concerned, Christianity had come between his brother and him. He didn't understand how that could be good, and truthfully he resented Kyle's new faith. From then on, they had an uneasy relationship right up to the night Kyle died.

After Kyle's death, Kelly's resentment seemed ridiculous and trivial. He agonized over the fact he'd let a philosophy get between them. Kelly did something else, too. Something he thought he owed his brother. He began to search for his own spiritual answers.

He also became close to Kyle's girlfriend, Brianna, the one person in the world who'd been there when it happened, who understood. She stayed close to Kelly whether he went on drinking binges or Bible-reading binges. Together they wrestled with the pain and tried to make sense of the tragedy.

Every day Brianna replayed the shooting. She often said, "He died with his arms around me," as though struggling to understand how Kyle could be sitting with his arm around her and in less than a second be dead. When Kelly drank, she stayed with him, but refused to drink herself.

One time she tried to kiss him, but then she pulled away and wiped her mouth. "You aren't Kyle," she simply said, as she stared into his face—a face so much like Kyle's.

Kelly hadn't understood at the time why Brianna and he couldn't talk about spiritual things. He assumed since she attended church and Christian concerts with Kyle that she understood spiritual matters. But, when he asked her about God, she always changed the subject. When he visited Pastor McDougal, she'd drift off to read a book or take a nap.

The September after Kyle's death, Kelly felt he stood on the edge of an emotional cliff. He'd heard that survivors sometimes couldn't bear the pain of loss, the guilt of surviving, the load of carrying on for someone else. He understood. He didn't know if he wanted to survive.

Desperate for answers, he called Pastor McDougal

and asked him to pray for him. Then he packed some food and a sleeping bag and disappeared into the mountains by himself for a few days. School had started and it was mid-week, so there were few campers and hikers around. Alone in the mountains he wrestled day and night with the pain that seared his soul, absorbed in his memories of Kyle. He cried out loud, wailing into the night as he went through every memory he had of Kyle. They'd shared a crib and later a room. They had made up their own special language, which only they could understand. He'd helped Kyle get through his challenges with math. Kyle helped him around school when he broke his leg. Without Kyle, he would never have learned to surf, but he'd taught his brother how to drive a car. Identical in looks, like an old married couple they knew each other's thoughts and finished each other's sentences.

There was no doubt, losing Kyle was like losing half of himself.

Suddenly, Kelly's mind came back to the present. He was at Cottonwood Creek, North Dakota, sitting under the starry sky. He jumped up and walked back into the house, as though he could walk away from the dark horror of Kyle's death. He locked the doors and flicked on the lights, trying to lock out thoughts of the past. It didn't work. Like a trance, scenes from the past gripped Kelly.

The last weeks of Kyle's life he'd seemed so upbeat, happy and confident, while Kelly himself had become increasingly more anxious and gloomy. Life seemed to overwhelm him at times.

Kyle had repeatedly told him that God was the answer, but Kelly ignored him. One time Kyle had pushed him against the wall and said, "God is the answer for you, Kelly, and I'm going to pray you are miserable until you get that figured out!"

After Kyle's death he was indeed miserable. Sometimes he felt like he was going insane, walking a tightrope over a deep canyon. One slip and....

That night in his isolated mountain camp, he'd decided he had three choices. He could continue his miserable walk on the tightrope. Or he could give up, become a beach bum or a mountain man and drink his life away. The third choice was to take Kyle's advice and try God. If he hadn't been so angry at the so-called "wonderful" God, the idea might have been more appealing. He figured he had every right to be angry. Even when Kyle was alive, God had come between them and then He had allowed Kyle to be blown away by a drunk.

Three torturing days and two sad, dark nights at his mountain camp passed before Kelly fell into a deep sleep, his anguish spent. On the third morning he awoke and squinted into a sky that must have looked like it did the first day of creation. The pale light of dawn reflected in the pristine lake. It occurred to him that the same scene had been recreated every day since the beginning of time. He lay transfixed, buried in his sleeping bag up to his neck, and watched the incredible light show evolve. A mist hung over far end of the lake, near a small waterfall. He could hear the water tinkling over the rocks, hear an occasional fish splash in the lake. Bands of brilliant pink, red and gold splayed out from the rising sun. To the north, mountains purpled with the morning light rose grandly to the heavens.

His three choices came to his mind, like dirty laundry in an immaculate room. He owed it to his parents not to live on the edge any more—if he died, they'd have double the grief and sadness. Neither could he continue to waste his life on alcohol, the very thing that led to Kyle's accidental death. In his mind he turned and faced the third choice.

"Lord, did you make all of this?" Kelly asked. The cool air seemed totally pure as he breathed it in. "Lord, life can't be some giant cosmic accident. I can't believe that any more. If someone made all of this, it had to be someone good and someone who is far smarter than humans.

"Lord I want to give you a try. I've been going along unthinkingly, but my brother Kyle, he thought it through and then he decided to follow you. Kyle...if Kyle believed in you, then I want to accept you as God of my life too. I don't have much to offer you at this point. I'm a big bag of confusion and pain. I don't understand, if you are so big and powerful, why you let Kyle die. He had his whole life ahead of him." A deep sadness overtook Kelly. The tears that sheeted down his face felt warm on his cold skin.

"He was so good. I don't understand why you let it happen, but I can't go on like this. If you are real and you want me, I'm yours."

As Kelly came to the end of the prayer, a feeling of peace began flowing through him from the top of his head all the way to his toes. He closed his eyes and breathed in. There was no way he could explain how the darkness lifted, but it had.

When he opened his eyes, he saw an eagle soar over the lake, higher and higher until it vanished into the vast purple mountain. "He's awesome, Lord, and he's sure of himself and he trusts you. I want to be like that eagle. He doesn't know what tomorrow will bring, but he's doing what he was made to do today."

Kelly went home later that week feeling like a new person. The sadness and loneliness still sometimes came back, but they came to visit, not to overwhelm him. For the first time his heart felt comforted. He'd spent even more time with Pastor McDougal after that. The Bible began to make more sense as he read it. He took several more trips into the mountains that fall seeking inspiration and solace.

In January, still not certain of what he wanted to do, he enrolled at a community college. The next spring Jim

Barnes introduced him to the idea of working at the summer camp. He applied to attend Bible college as soon as he got back from his summer in North Dakota.

Kelly's mind once again returned to the living room of his new home at Cottonwood Creek.

"Jim Barnes, you had no idea of what you were starting," Kelly said aloud again, a big smile on his face. He glanced out the living room window. The orange ball of sun had vanished, while he relived the past. Once upstairs he looked out the bedroom window and noted the night was as black as a mountain camp ground. Ah, he thought, no street lights. He looked up at the night sky. The stars had never seemed so bright, nor could he remember ever seeing so many. Might be time to take up astronomy, he thought. A big yawn escaped him and he realized how tired he was. However, before crawling into bed, he paused for a moment with one last thought of his brother.

"Kyle, with the help of God I will do everything in my power to fill up the next years enough for the two of us," Kelly pledged. "And Lord, my God, I bless your name and thank you for all you've done for me. Just thinking about the past makes me realize what you saved me from. And it makes me wonder what you will do in my life. I give it all to you, the past, the present and the future."

Chapter 2

Kelly awoke to the sound of birds singing the next morning and felt around for his watch. It was 5 a.m. In California it was 3 a.m. He moaned and pulled the covers over his head. A moment later he got up and shut the bedroom window, but didn't think to draw the heavy drapes. An hour later the room was so bright with sun light that he woke again. This time he got up and showered, then went down to the kitchen.

He poured himself some orange juice and opened the back door to see what the morning looked like. No newspaper on the step. He thought of his father, who had stepped outside almost every morning of his adult life to pick up the morning newspaper. Kelly doubted whether newspapers were delivered in the country. However, he did find a hungry cat, who happily came inside with him. He noted that her fur was clean and he wondered if she had spent the night bathing.

He poured her a bowl of milk and dropped pieces of bread in it, like he'd seen his mother do for a stray cat one time. The kitty gobbled it all up, so he gave her some sandwich meat. He made himself a piece of toast and gave her one, also, and she ate it.

"I'm glad you aren't a fussy eater," he said. "My bachelor cooking isn't so great."

The phone rang at 7:12 a.m. and Kelly caught it on the first ring.

"Pastor, this is Maury Jackson. Hope I didn't wake you."

"Not at all," said Kelly as he eyed the cat, who was

running a damp paw over her milky whiskers.

"Well, that's good. I need to talk to you today and I took the liberty of setting up meetings with the organist and the Sunday school superintendent. I hope you don't mind."

"Oh that's good. I'm grateful," said Kelly. "Would you like to drive out this morning?"

"Yes, if that's all right, I'll be over around 9 a.m."

Kelly hung up the phone and stepped in the cat's bowl. She had licked it dry, but she was nowhere to be seen.

"Where'd you go Madam? Madam? Hey, I'm not going to play hide and seek with you!" Of course, he did, looking everywhere he could think for the cat, but she'd vanished inside the house.

Finally Kelly gave up the hunt and hurried across the footbridge to the church. He marveled at how it gleamed in the morning sun. Its wood frame seemed newly painted. The vestibule on the north side was a fairly recent addition and contained a long ramp to the basement, built to accommodate wheelchairs. Up a half dozen stairs, the church sanctuary was cool, with dazzling light filtering through the stained glass windows. The sanctuary held 120 people and had been full the day Kelly interviewed.

He walked up to the altar area and looked down at the pews. To his left was an organ and to his right a piano. Short pews served as choir seating, although no choir had sung the Sunday he had been here to candidate.

The communion table was set in front of the altar. A white tablecloth with some kind of needlework covered it. He reached out his hand and touched the luminous brass cross that sat on the table next to a large Bible opened to the third chapter of John.

Kelly went through the side door into a small room that led outside. He supposed that nervous grooms waited here, or Christmas pageant angels or pastors who wanted to make a grand entrance. Kelly didn't think he'd use it. He walked back down the center aisle and made his way to the basement. The main room could be divided by curtains to form classrooms. The restrooms were at the back, near the kitchen. For the first time Kelly noticed the church was built on a slope that allowed a door leading outside from the basement.

Somewhere a phone started ringing. He began to look for it and finally found it on the fifth ring in the kitchen on the far side of an ancient refrigerator.

"Cottonwood Church, Pastor Jorgenson speaking. How can I help you?"

"Hi Kelly, it's me, Bri. You sound so professional."

"Yeah, right, I just had a marathon hunt for the phone!" he replied, leaning back against the counter. "You're up pretty early. It can't be 7 a.m. in Frisco."

"I talked to your mom late last evening and she said you made it to North Dakota just fine. I'm sorry I wasn't home when you called last night. We had an evening event, a wine-tasting party to welcome a new artist," said Brianna.

"Yeah, I tried calling you, but I was too tired to keep trying. Listen Bri, you should see the house, it's so cool. It was built in 1926 and it's filled with all kinds of neat windows and woodwork."

"Sounds quaint, Kelly. Did you get all moved in?"

"I had lots of help moving in. A whole bunch of people showed. They brought a picnic supper and helped unload furniture. I still have a lot of boxes to unpack, but first I need to get up to speed on the church stuff. I give my first sermon on Sunday as pastor and this is already Thursday. I really didn't decide on a subject until last evening, so I have some research and writing to do."

"Sounds like you will be busy for a while."

"Bri, I really wish you could be here and share this

whole new part of my life with me. Is there any way you can come up here?"

"Not now. I'll come with your folks in September. Remember I'm starting a new job, too."

"Yeah, I know. And I'm not there for all of your new experiences either. What would we do without phones?"

"Listen Sweetie, I need to get to work. Call me tonight. No wait, I have plans tonight. Call me tomorrow, okay?"

"Will do. Love you, Bri."

"Love you, too. Bye."

Just as the phone disconnected, Kelly saw Maury drive up to the parsonage. Kelly hurried through the newly-discovered door in the basement and over to the house. He wanted to think about his relationship with Brianna, but there wasn't time. He wanted to stop and enjoy the perfect morning, but there wasn't time. He wanted to find that sneaky cat, but there wasn't time. And it was only his first day on the job.

"Morning, Maury," Kelly said as he strode across the yard.

"Pastor, I see you're up and at it," said Maury as they walked into the house. "You wouldn't happen to have a spare cup of coffee would you?"

"Well, if I remember correctly, I have a coffee pot and some coffee, but I don't drink the stuff and don't know how to make it."

"Let me do the honors, then," said Maury. Kelly found the pot and coffee in a box. Maury took off his cowboy hat and tossed it on the washer in the entry, then showed Kelly how to make coffee.

"You might want to acquire a taste for the stuff. Hospitality and drinking coffee are one and the same around here. You offer it to anyone who comes to visit and it's a sign of friendship to drink a cup or two together."

"I'll make a stab at drinking it, although I'm a soda

pop man," said Kelly as he searched through a couple boxes looking for cups. "And I'll take your advice and offer
coffee to anyone who stops by."

The men spent the next two hours discussing the upcoming church service, the people responsible for each
part and the board meeting set to take place the following Tuesday. Maury reminded him the church had run
smoothly for several months without a pastor and while
his leadership would be very important in the future, it
was all right for Kelly to ease himself into it. Still, Kelly
felt much better informed and ready to take charge of the
church by the time Maury left.

Later, Kelly looked around the house for the cat again,
but couldn't locate her. He spilled the rest of his coffee in
the sink, made himself a sandwich and popped open a soft
drink. He began putting his dishes, pots and pan into the
cupboards while he ate. After lunch, he got in his pickup
and drove the 10 miles over to Schulteville, the home of his
second parish, Cross Church.

Schulteville was so small, if you were daydreaming
you could drive right through it and not know you'd been
there. He easily found the soft yellow Queen Anne style
home where one of the most prominent church members
lived. The house was across the street from the church. Before he got to the front porch, the door whipped opened.

"Pastor Kelly! Land's sake, it's good to see you! How
was your trip to Dakota? Come in here. Marge, we have
company, get out the silver tea set!"

Kelly felt like he'd just met a whirlwind instead of
Kate Schulte, a white-haired lady of 85. Kate dragged him
inside the house before he could say a word.

"Lovely day outside. I hope you get out and get some
fresh air instead of spending all day visiting old ladies," she
said, a strange clicking sound accompanying her words.
Dentures, Kelly thought. His grandmother had talked the

same way. "Did I tell you to call me Aunt Kate? 'Tis what everyone else in Cottonwood County calls me. You might as well, too." By now, Kate had stuffed Kelly into a chair slip-covered in yellow cotton.

"They're all waiting for me to die," she continued to his surprise. "So far I've fooled them. I'm too ornery to die," she said with a wide smile.

"Aunt Kate, you need to treat Pastor Kelly better if you want him to come around once in awhile," scolded a woman with trim gray hair. Kelly recognized Marge Selby as she stood in the living room doorway, a dish towel in her hand. He remembered she and her husband, Wayne, had moved in with Kate and her brother to help care for them.

"Welcome!" she said, turning to Kelly. "Can I get you some lemonade?"

"Sure. Thank you, Marge," he said, relieved for the intervention. That was another piece of advice both Maury and Tiny had given him: if you are offered food or something to drink, always accept. Marge disappeared and in a moment reappeared with a tray holding a pitcher of lemonade, glasses and a plate of sugar cookies.

Aunt Kate looked out the front window. A couple of kids were riding bikes on the gravel street.

"They'll never amount to anything," she said, nodding toward the kids. "Need some good sound lickings to keep them in line."

Kelly's eyebrows shot up in surprise again at her unexpected comment. He wondered if he could end up with a permanent surprised look on his face.

"Honestly, Aunt Kate, I never know what will come out of your mouth," said Marge, as she sat down. "Are you getting settled, Pastor?" she asked, turning her attention to Kelly.

"Sort of. I've unpacked a couple boxes," said Kelly,

finding his voice again. "I just wanted to touch base with you about Sunday. I plan to be here by 8:45 a.m. if that sounds all right to you."

"That's fine," said Marge. "We'll have everything ready for the service." From his previous visit, he knew Marge and her husband, Wayne, pretty much kept Cross Church open. His main job was to preach the sermon.

"We probably won't have as many people as last time you were here," said Aunt Kate. Ten people had attended the service when he gave his trial sermon. "They're all away on vacation," she said with a wave of her white hanky.

"Now that's not true. We seldom have many people," said Marge. "Our little town is dying and I'm sorry to say our little church is, too. I don't know if anyone has told you, but since you were here, Aunt Kate's brother Ted was in the hospital and now is in a nursing home in Bismarck."

"He'll be back," said Aunt Kate, emphatically. "And if we can get the café and the school reopened, the rest of the town will boom."

"I'm sorry to hear about Ted. Perhaps I can visit him when I go to Bismarck," Kelly said. Marge smiled encouragingly at him. Kate frowned, but her eyes said she appreciated his idea.

"When did the café close?" Kelly asked, innocently, thinking that it must have been a recent event.

"'Twas just before Labor Day. Or was it just after Labor Day? In 1983," said Aunt Kate, nodding her head.

Kelly's eyebrows, which had finally relaxed, went up again. That was 18 years ago!

"Three things you need in a town—a church, a school and a café. The rest can come later. We've done everything we can to keep the church open, but nobody else is willing to do their part!" Kate was almost shouting. "It's time for people in this town to wake up and smell the coffee!"

Kelly finally found a graceful time to leave and Marge

walked him to the street.

"Wow!" is all he could say.

"She's pretty eccentric," Marge giggled. "But inside she's a real softy. She knows the town her father founded is dying out and she can't do much about it. We try to keep that in mind when she's difficult."

"Which must be a lot of the time," said Kelly as he studied Marge's face. She smiled and nodded silently.

"As difficult as she can be, Wayne and I both feel that this is where God wants us. There is no one else to care for her."

"Marge, I think you deserve a medal," said Kelly. He took her hand and gave it a squeeze.

When Kelly returned to the parsonage, he heard the cat meowing. He searched the first floor, and then went upstairs. At the bathroom door he stopped as the sound grew louder. Pulling back the vanity skirt he peered under the sink.

"Oh no!" he said as he surveyed the scene. The cat was lying on its side, surrounded by a batch of kittens. Kneeling down, he could hear her begin to purr, as though she was proud to show off her new brood. It appeared there were four kittens in the litter.

"Oh, no!" Kelly said again. "Lord, I'm holding you responsible for this situation. And you Lady Kitty, why did you have to pick my house?" He rubbed the cat's head and gingerly touched the kittens.

Then he heard noise downstairs and someone yelling, "Anybody home?" Kelly hurried down the steps. The mailman stood in the middle of the kitchen. Two small, heavy boxes which Kelly had shipped lay on the counter. After introductions, he explained that there were two large boxes waiting at the post office, but he didn't have room in his car to deliver them. Kelly looked at his watch and decided he just had enough time to drive to town and retrieve the boxes before the post office closed for the day. He could also pick up some kitty supplies before the stores closed.

He sped off, realizing he didn't even know where the post office was. Not a problem, he found out. When he arrived in town, he met Mavis Jackson driving up Main Street.

Mavis slowed when she spied him. He stopped and rolled down the pickup window. Mavis gave him directions to the Post Office, and then insisted he stop by for dinner.

"Mavis, that sounds so good, but the truth is I've hardly started unpacking or preparing a sermon for Sunday."

"Tell you what," she responded, "dinner will be ready in 30 minutes and as soon as it's over, you are free to leave. We're thinking of taking in a movie over in Garrison, anyway."

"It's a deal." Kelly picked up the parcels at the post office and bought some cat food at the grocery store. Then he stopped at the hardware store for a litter box and made it to the Jackson's home right on time. A small black sports car sat out front.

When he knocked on the door, Maury answered it. "Glad you could make it. I want to introduce you to our daughter, Linda. She just surprised us by coming home for a long weekend." Linda gave him a tight little smile and continued setting the table. Although she might have been attractive, she wore no makeup and appeared to cut her own hair. She wore a shapeless long shift and sandals.

Maury and Mavis tried very hard to interest Kelly and Linda in each other during dinner. Kelly learned that Linda was 24 and lived about 150 miles away in Grand Forks. She was working on her doctorate and taught psychology at a state university. Beyond that she volunteered very little information.

"Say wasn't there a bad flood in Grand Forks a few years ago?" Kelly asked, trying to steer the conversation away from personal information and acquaint himself with the area.

"Yes, much of the city was flooded in 1997," Mavis said. "Thousands of people were out of their homes. And to make matters worse, the central part of the city caught fire in the midst of the flood."

"That's quite a story," Kelly said in sympathy. Life seemed to be so harsh on the Plains. "How is the city doing now?"

"They've recovered quite nicely," Maury said. "Everyone worked and helped pull things together and rebuild the city. It's an incredible story."

When they finished, Mavis suggested Kelly and Linda take a walk to the Dairy Cone for dessert, scooting them out of the house like two children, Kelly thought. Still he sensed that he shouldn't decline, so he stood and nodded at Linda. "I think a walk is a great idea after such a good meal," he said.

They were hardly out the door, when Linda became more talkative.

"You are a spiritual person," she said.

"I hope so—I am a pastor."

"You've been through a very dark period, but you've come into the light."

"What makes you think that?" Kelly asked.

"I'm into spiritual things, too. My parents aren't aware of my beliefs. They'd never understand. They're so traditional. They don't understand it is a new age and there are new things to connect with."

"I'm not sure I understand. I'm into contemporary Christian music..."

Linda laughed. "That's not what I mean."

When Kelly shook his head, Linda rolled her eyes.

"You went to seminary and all they taught you was about God, right? Did they teach you anything about the Goddess?"

"What goddess?"

"Don't you know? There are big conferences going on all over, introducing her to people who find a strictly masculine god unacceptable. I feel that I also have come into the light and a new understanding of spirituality."

"Oh, I see. A bunch of women who don't want to submit to a male savior, so they invent their own god," said Kelly. His own words startled him and he immediately wished he'd been silent. Linda glared at him.

"I'm sorry, I shouldn't have said that," said Kelly. "I investigated a lot of beliefs before accepting Christianity."

"You know I really would rather we end this discussion," Linda said, spinning around and heading back to her parent's house. The atmosphere had grown about as icy as it could get in June, Kelly decided. When they arrived at the house, Kelly stuck his head inside the door and thanked Mavis for the meal again, then quickly left.

As he drove back to his home, Kelly could feel the muscles in his face tightening. The day started out great with a phone call from Brianna and a good meeting with Maury, but his encounters since then had been decidedly unhappy. First, he felt like a mouse being played with by a cat when he went to see the cantankerous Kate Schulte. Then a stray cat had kittens in his bathroom. Kelly could feel the blood coursing through the veins in his temple. And now a tangle with a goddess worshiper, who just happened to be the daughter of two very sweet people, who were obviously trying to do some match making.

"Whatever made me think life might be simpler up here on the Plains?" Kelly wondered out loud. "Less traffic and people, certainly, but just as many problems. I don't know if I'm mature or wise enough to handle all this. I take that back: I know I'm not wise enough to deal with this avalanche.

"Lord, I confess, I'm discouraged by some of the things that happened today. Your Word says that you give wisdom to those who need it. And I need your wisdom, your discernment and your peace and whatever else you have for me."

It wasn't until he prayed that Kelly realized he hadn't spent any real time in prayer all day. Quick prayers, meal prayers, but not a time set apart to thank, praise and worship and do some Bible reading.

"Lord, I'm sorry I haven't spent much time with you the last couple days. It's been busy, but when I'm too busy to spend time with you, there is something wrong. Please forgive me."

Kelly parked in front of the house and took the supplies inside. Upstairs he found the cat and kittens contently sleeping under his bathroom sink.

"First things first, Madam," he addressed the cat as he began to move her and her family. "If you're going to live with me, you need a name. I'm going to call you Mildred after one of my favorite high school teachers, because your fur is gray and her hair was gray. So, Mildred, you and your family are moving into the little room across the hall. You will have a nice box, kitty litter, water and food. If you need anything else, please let me know."

Mildred turned around a couple times and then settled in with the kittens, so Kelly headed for the church for some quality prayer time. He had strolled to the footbridge between the parsonage and the church before he heard the music. He noticed a white vehicle partially hidden by the building. Kelly wondered if he had forgotten a meeting and quickened his pace.

Kelly opened the church door and moved noiselessly to the door of the sanctuary. The sun streamed through the west windows bathing the room in gold. A shimmering brightness danced over every surface. The cross on the altar shone brighter than anything else, but even the wooden pews took on an ethereal look. The stained-glass windows reflected rainbow colors that splashed across the high ceiling. Kelly felt he'd just opened a door and walked into heaven.

A strong sense of peace washed over him. As his eyes became accustomed to the bright light, he saw a young woman with curly golden hair. She sat with her back to him at the piano, singing a love song to God as her hands flowed gently over the keys.

"Draw me close to you, Lord. Never let me go. You are my desire. No one else will do. You're all I want, you're all I ever needed. You're all I want Lord, help me know you are near." The last note lingers in the air.

Then she turned and Kelly realized he must have made a sound that caught her attention.

"You sing and play beautifully," he said. "Please don't let me disturb you."

She was silent for a moment and Kelly saw the color rise in her cheeks.

"I'm Kelly Jorgenson, the new pastor."

She stood up and started moving toward him.

"You're welcome to come here any time. I'll try not to intrude again."

By now she was face to face with him and he thought maybe it was the dazzling golden light, but she had the most angelic face he'd ever seen.

"It is the one place where I can go and pour my heart out to God," she whispered, as she whisked past.

"Please continue," Kelly started to say, but she had already slipped past him. "I mean, continue now and always feel welcome to come back. Any time."

Then she turned and looked directly into his eyes. He

felt as though she could see right into his heart, yet kindness filled her eyes.

"There is power in the name of Jesus and there is power in the Word of God," she said softly. "But when you praise his holy name, something more happens. The glory of all heaven joins you."

Kelly stood speechless as she vanished through the door. In seconds a car engine started.

Too stunned to follow her, he sank into a nearby pew. What did she mean? Was it a message from God to him? Was she an angel? No, her hand was as soft as kitten fur. She is real, he thought, with a strange stirring in his heart. But who is she?

The brilliant light began to fade, but Kelly remained immersed in the holiness of the moment, pondering what had just taken place. He felt totally unworthy of this gift. The day had been so frustrating and God had seemed so far away. Yet now, Kelly sensed the comfort of His presence in the sanctuary.

"Oh Father, I have let things crowd into my life and steal the precious time I need to spend with you. Time that I want to spend with you. Oh, forgive me for letting the urgent fill my life, rather than the important. Thank you for this moment. I praise your name. Thank you for being faithful to me. Thank you for offering me fresh insight into what you have for me and for this church. Lord, I praise you that you can be found on the prairie as well as in Bible camps and schools and in the mountains. Thank you most of all for new beginnings and that you are always ready to help your people—help me—find the way."

Peace filled the golden sanctuary and Kelly lingered long after night arrived.

Chapter 3

A quick look in the rearview mirror as she backed her white Jeep out of the church yard showed Amber Rose McLean that she'd blushed crimson with embarrassment that someone had invaded her private moment. Someone young and handsome.

She'd often stopped at the unlocked church. The place had become a refuge from the unrelenting demands made on her. No one knew about her occasional spiritual rendezvous until now. Amber didn't like being caught in an unguarded moment. She never let her mask down for a minute, for fear of crumbling. She couldn't afford that.

Cruising slowly back to the farm with the window open, she took in the dusky sights and sounds. A meadowlark sat on a fence post serenading the coming night. A family of ducks swam in a slough beside the road. Crickets thrrrped in tall prairie grass. Country life flowed in her veins and she relished these quiet interludes.

Back at the farm, she shut off the engine and sat for a moment. Her brothers, Adam who was 19, and Daniel, 17, were in the shop helping their father, Glen, repair the hay mower. The wide door was open and light glowed from it as a drill whined somewhere within. The twins were pitching a softball back and forth under the yard light. Amber had hoped to find them in the bathtub. The house was dark. With a twinge of guilt nipping at her conscience, she tried to justify her escape from kitchen duty. The others could help, too, she thought. Not everything had to rest on her shoulders.

"Tim and Jim," she called as she climbed from the

car, "why aren't you getting ready for bed? In the house, on the double!" The 10-year-old boys raced wildly around the farm yard and eventually, just before she lost her temper, arrived at the door of the house holding out a box to her.

"What's this?"

"A present," said Jim, innocently.

"Yeah, right. What is it—a snake? A mouse?" The twins exchanged looks, and then Tim said, "We're just trying to be nice! Open it."

Amber opened the box. A small frog looked up at her. She glared at her brothers who bounded up the steps to the house. After scooping the frog out of the box and setting it in some grass, she followed the boys into the house and into the tiny bathroom.

"Clothes in the hamper! Both of you wash that dirty hair of yours! If you don't, I'll come in and wash it myself," she said. Catching a whiff of the peculiar smell of dirt and sweat that permeates little boys on hot summer days, she rolled her eyes and left the room.

Amber crossed the kitchen and went into the tiny living room.

"Mom, you're up pretty late. How are you feeling?" she asked, clicking on a ceramic table lamp.

"It's definitely one of my better days, but I probably should get back in bed."

Amber released the brake on the wheelchair and pushed her mother into the small main-floor bedroom. She helped the 46-year-old woman change into a nightgown and brushed her hair. After the twins left the bathroom and came in for quick "good-nights," she helped her mother back into wheelchair for a trip to the bathroom.

The whole house grew quiet once her mother and the twins settled down for the night. Adam and Danny were in the basement playing computer games and her father was engrossed in the newspaper.

This was the worst time of day for Amber, the time when she should be out on a date or snuggling with a husband. Her friend, Sandy, kept saying Amber needed a life.

Amber knew the truth was she'd probably never have "a life" of her own. Her parents needed her to help raise the rest of their family. It wasn't easy for them. Because of the farm economy and bad weather, they'd lost money two years in a row now. Her father was a hard worker and he raised a breed of Angus cattle that his grandfather had brought from Scotland decades before. His cattle were known throughout the United States and he'd gained the respect of his German and Norwegian neighbors. Respect didn't pay the bills however, and for now the cattle market was down. Way down. None of them talked about the possibility of selling out. Their family had lived on this same farm since 1902 and her father was too stubborn to consider leaving it, but how long could they survive without an income?

All of this was bad enough without her mother's medical bills. Amber could still remember her mother as a healthy woman, singing to the twins when they were infants and spreading sunshine wherever she went. Shortly after their birth, however, Jean was diagnosed with multiple sclerosis. At first she had small bouts of the disease and long periods of remission, but that gradually changed. Now she was either in bed or in a wheelchair. She could still read and do small things with her hands, but even those actions were becoming more limited.

Amber admired her mother. She did her best to make sure the kids went to school in clean clothes and did their homework. Jean knew her brood of children well and wisely guided their lives. She rarely pitied herself and spent many hours in prayer.

"The devil can steal away my body, but he can't have my soul or my love for God," she often said. When she was up to it, Glen took her to church; however it had now been months since Jean had been able to attend. Glen refused to go without her.

Although it was 10 p.m., Amber went to the kitchen, pulled a bowl out of the cupboard and started mixing up some cookies. At 13, Amber began taking over kitchen duties for her mother and by the time she was out of high school, she did much of the work around the house.

As the valedictorian of her class, she'd dreamed of going to college. She'd asked God to help her get an education, but since it seemed like such a remote possibility, she'd cried herself to sleep many nights. Not only was she needed at home, there wasn't an extra dime to put toward tuition.

One August day after her high school graduation, Amber had walked down the driveway to the mailbox and found a large envelope addressed to her. In it was a full scholarship to attend one of the best private colleges in the state. At first she thought it was a mistake. Once she realized it was her open door to a college education, she laughed and then cried. It took her a full day to tell her parents about the scholarship, because she feared her secret dream of attending college might be snuffed out by circumstances.

"This is too wonderful, but I can't go. Who would do laundry? Who would make dinner? And pack lunches? And make the twins mind? And buy groceries? And shop for school clothes?" she asked her parents.

But they insisted that she go. "Letting you go is our gift to you," her father had said. "It's time the other kids pick up some of chores that you do around here."

After inquiring, she learned that her high school accounting teacher had applied to the college for Amber. Each year the college gave out one full scholarship to a deserving student and that year it was Amber. A true answer to her prayer, Amber believed.

The first year at college was hard. Amber hadn't known a single person on campus. She didn't have a car and she wore her clothes from high school. Still, she really didn't mind, because she was living a dream come true. By the end of that first year, she'd made several good friends, including Sandy. She'd gotten some part-time jobs so she had a little spending money. She went home every week-end possible and picked up her responsibilities there.

The years flew by and on her 22nd birthday she'd graduated with a degree in business management. She'd transferred from the insurance agency where she worked near the college to a sister agency in Bismarck, which was closer to Cottonwood City.

She loved her work and was able to travel to the farm more frequently. A year later one of the partners left the agency and the others invited her to take his accounts. It was a rare opportunity for someone so young and she jumped at the chance. Often she put in 50 to 60 hours a week at the business, then spent the weekend helping on the farm. She had bought the shiny, new Jeep and furnished her apartment, then started putting any extra money she had back into the family, paying the kids' dental bills, buying school clothes or whatever else they needed.

"You have no life," her friend Sandy told her in their frequent phone calls.

"I have too much of a life to have a real life," Amber responded each time. The truth was she felt trapped. She loved her family too much to desert them and the only thing she could do was sacrifice her personal life.

She often mixed up a batch of cookies late at night. As far as Amber could tell, there weren't any changes coming in the future. Long ago she began trying to trust God for tomorrow and concentrate on making the best of each new day.

Still, her heart longed for more and as she mixed the cookie dough, her thoughts turned to the new, young pastor at Cottonwood Church.

Chapter 4

On Saturday, Kelly viewed the yard with a critical eye. Grass didn't grow nearly so fast or high in Southern California. Then he realized it was his job to mow the yard around the church and parsonage. He got out an aging lawn tractor and fiddled with it until it began running smoothly, thankful it wasn't a push type. Then around and around he rode, glad for the time it gave him time to practice his sermon aloud, the sweet smell of new mown grass filling the air.

He started out quietly, as though someone might overhear him, but soon enough began practicing his strong pulpit voice. "The title of today's sermon is 'The God of New Beginnings.' The Bible is peppered with stories of how God gave his people opportunities to start over. Sometimes they needed a new start because of sad or troubled experiences and sometimes because of sin in their lives. We're often the same way—we need a fresh start.

"The book of Ruth tells the story of God helping two poor women who needed a new beginning. When their husbands died, Naomi and her daughter-in-law Ruth traveled back to Naomi's homeland. There, God gave them new hope and a fresh start. In that destitute time, when they cast their future on God, neither of them could know all God had stored up for them. In fact, Ruth became an ancestor of our Lord Jesus."

Kelly paused as he completed the parsonage yard. He went back to the garage and filled the mower's gas tank. Someone had thoughtfully left it full. He wheeled out to the road and over to the church lawn. Then he continued practicing his sermon. "The story of David, found in I and

II Samuel, is quite different. The Bible describes David as a man after God's own heart. He did mighty things for his God, beginning with slaying the giant Goliath. He ruled a mighty kingdom for God, but then he fell from grace. David had an adulterous affair and tried to cover it up. He had the woman's husband killed. Two grave sins. Yet, when he repented, God forgave him and restored him. There is another lesson here: even great men of God are human and can make mistakes—big ones. That is why we must pray for our Christian leaders. The mightier they are, the more we need to cover them in prayer.

"The book of Acts in the New Testament tells of a very religious man who thought he was helping God out by killing the early Christians. That is, until the risen Jesus appeared to him. After that, Saul turned his life around and became a slave to Jesus Christ and the world's greatest missionary. God gave him a new beginning. He even gave him a new name. We now know Saul as the Apostle Paul.

"Do you need a new beginning today? Have circumstances stolen your hope? Have you fallen into sin? If so, don't despair! Jesus told us in Matthew 18: 22 that we are to continue to forgive each other, even if we must do it 70 times seven. That is a clue as to how many times the Lord is willing to forgive us.

"One of the eternal truths of the Bible is found in Jeremiah 29: 11: 'For I know the plans I have for you, declares the Lord, plans to prosper you and not to harm you, plans to give you hope and a future.'"

"If you need a new beginning today, bow your heads with me as we ask God to help us move forward into the rich blessing he has for each of us."

Satisfied with the message, he decided to let it simmer in his heart for a while and then work on it again before going to bed. Meanwhile, back and forth he went, up and down, sweeping the tall, green grass under the mower.

Soon his thoughts turned to some of the people who were now part of his new life.

Kelly had liked Maury Jackson right away when he'd flown to North Dakota as a candidate for the job several weeks earlier. Maury, in his tall hat and genuine cowboy boots, and Tiny Winger, wearing his work cap, had been at the airport in Bismarck to meet him. They'd picked him out of a crowd of over a hundred people who got off the plane that day. When Kelly expressed his surprise, having never met them before, Maury had slapped him on the shoulder and said, "Horse sense. You need to have horse sense to live out here."

Maury was of medium build, but had the thick muscular arms of a man used to heavy farm work. His brown hair was permeated with gray. He had a "rubbery" face that expressed itself so well, that Kelly doubted the man ever played poker. When he laughed, his whole face crinkled up and his brown eyes became little slits.

Tiny, on the other hand, wasn't tiny at all. When Tiny smiled, his full-moon face lit up. He was 32 and managed the convenience store, gas station and auto repair shop in Cottonwood City. Tiny was very proud that he had expanded the business in the few years since he'd taken it over from his father. He employed two clerks for the store and a mechanic for the shop. He did a lot of the mechanical work himself, along with keeping the books.

Maury and Tiny had entertained Kelly with one story after another on the drive from Bismarck to Cottonwood City. As they drove along Highway 83, they had pointed out all the features of the land, until Kelly thought the state tourism department should hire them. The Missouri River, often visible from the four-lane highway, awed Kelly. It was wide and filled with sandbars. They pointed out the Lewis & Clark Interpretive Center north of Washburn and then the tremendous power plants that dot the state.

"See up here?" asked Maury. "We're going to drive across the lake that was made when the Missouri was dammed, back in the early 1950s. On your left is Lake Sakakawea, but this here highway divides it from Lake Audubon.

"Yes, sir, when they dammed up the Missouri, it sure changed a lot of things. It hasn't flooded since the 1950s. That really helped Bismarck grow. And the amount of power generated at the dam is incredible. Great fishing at the lake. Have you ever fished for lake salmon?"

"Ah, no," replied Kelly. "Sounds like something I'd like to try."

"Well the last pastor left a fishing boat behind your garage. The lake is 200 miles long and the waves get pretty big," said Maury. "The boat is pretty small so you'd best fish in some of the coves. Or better yet, try Lake Audubon. It's smaller. If you decide to take the boat out, make sure you take someone with you who knows the lakes."

"That'd be me or Maury," added Tiny with a grin.

Kelly's first trip to the town of Cottonwood City that day in May had included the 120-mile round trip to and from the airport, giving two sermons and being interviewed by both church boards, all in 24 hours.

After arriving at the town, they'd driven out to Cottonwood Church and met with the board. He'd had a quick tour of the parsonage where he would be living. Mavis had dinner waiting when the men arrived back at Cottonwood City.

The next morning they'd driven him to Cross Church in Schulteville, his second congregation. He'd met with their board, toured the church, met the people, gave a sermon and immediately left to give a sermon at Cottonwood Church. George and Bonnie Jackson, Maury's brother and sister-in-law, invited him and the other board members for Sunday dinner. Later Maury and Tiny drove him back to the airport at Bismarck to catch the afternoon flight to California.

The time spent in North Dakota had seemed like a whirlwind and Kelly didn't know how they could even make up their minds about him. Yet, a week later Maury had called and said the two congregations had met and agreed to invite him to be their pastor. Kelly knew before Maury ever mentioned a salary, that he would accept. Something in him longed for the solid people he'd met at Cottonwood Creek and their way of life. Kelly felt his youth, mentally as well as spiritually, but he had a deep sense that God would help him minister to these people.

Chapter 5

For several weeks the weather remained dry and the grassy pastures changed from lime green to grassy green to golden. Farmers pushed their caps back and evaluated whether the heat would hurt or help the crops. Finally thunderstorms rumbled across the prairie one July night. An all-day drizzle followed. It kept Maury and George Jackson out of the field and gave them an unexpected day off. The brothers called Kelly that morning and invited him to come out for the day. They planned to give him a crash course in the agricultural business.

Kelly admired the white buildings as he drove into the farm yard. Each had a green roof. The white fencing appeared freshly painted. Dense shelter belts protectively circled three sides of the farm. Many of the trees were loaded with plums, chokecherries or apples.

Kelly thought the scene was picture perfect. He spied George and Maury through the door of a machine shed. They appeared to be working on a piece of equipment, so he drove up to the building and parked.

"Hey, young fellow, I hope you're here to lend a hand," Maury greeted Kelly, as he climbed out of the pickup and strode to the building.

"Yes, I imagine I could fix that piece of machinery pretty good for you," Kelly responded. Kyle had been the more mechanical of the twins, something that Kelly tried to overcome. Getting the lawnmower running every week was close to the peak of his mechanical ability.

"That was a good come back," said George. "Maury better take you up on it."

"I have a better idea," said Maury. "Let's go see if we can scare up some coffee in the house."

"This weather," said Maury, shaking his head as they walked through the drizzle. "Comes a day every July when things quit growing toward their potential and begin their downward spiral. By fall, plants, trees and grass are drying out and getting ready to rest for the winter. Summer's half over, Pastor Kelly. My favorite half is over for another year."

The low-roofed 1970s ranch house belonged to George, but Kelly noted that Maury seemed equally comfortable in it.

"He better be," George said. "Bonnie quit perking coffee for us a long time ago and he doesn't like the way I make it." He shook some cookies out of a bag onto a plate.

"Well, this is George's house, but it's setting on my land," responded Maury, who lived in town.

"Our land."

"Our grandfather homesteaded here around the turn of the century," continued Maury. "He literally broke the sod with a hand-guided plow and oxen. By the time we came along 50 years later, he and Dad had expanded the acreage considerably."

"Life has changed out here so much, you wouldn't recognize it anymore," said George. "We aren't farmers, we're agricultural engineers. You have to specialize to make it anymore. You invest a quarter million dollars here and a quarter million there, then you hope and pray you get your money out of it."

"So you two are specialized, but in different things," said Kelly, helping himself to a chocolate chip cookie.

"That's right," said Maury. "George has a contract with the French fry potato plant in Jamestown to supply potatoes to them. He spent a quarter million installing irrigation, by the way. The second big stash of cash went to investing in the processing and hauling equipment.

"I grow canola and am part of an oil processing co-op located about 30 miles from here. 'Course I like to keep a few animals around, so I've been breeding miniature horses."

"Which I have to feed when we get a good blizzard," added George.

"Yeah, unless you're lucky enough to have me stranded out here during the storm, so I can lose a few pinochle games to you," joshed Maury. He had set three mugs of coffee on the round oak kitchen table. Someone had covered the table with a familiar-looking red checked tablecloth, Kelly noted.

"This is all new to me, but I want learn about life out here," said Kelly, seriously. "It appears to me that, although you are both successful, there are a lot of people struggling to make ends meet. What are you up against out here?"

"Well, we're up against the weather, low prices, high costs, lack of jobs in town, an uncertain future and a lot of traditional thinking," replied George. "The odds are against us. In fact, there is a saying in the ag industry, that you can start farming if you have a million dollars and you can keep farming until it's all gone."

"But I don't understand," said Kelly. "I kind of pictured farms to look like Old McDonald's farm. It's really pretty out here, but it's anything but the simple life I pictured."

"Well, let's start back in the 1950s," said George, as he poured more coffee in the cups and set the pot back on the coffee maker.

"When we were growing up there were twice as many farms around here. Most of them had nice-sized families. No one worked in town, like today. We depend on Bonnie's check from working at the bank and the money Mavis makes teaching music. Most people have at least one off-farm income. In fact, around here a lot of the men work at the power plants or the mines. They farm in their spare time.

"But back then we had a flock of chickens and milked a dozen cows. Ma sold cream and eggs in town to pay for groceries. We had a few hogs or sheep. Every year we'd plant corn, wheat and millet. We'd raise hay and oats to feed the cattle. Pretty self sufficient."

"Yeah," Maury joined in. "Ma raised chickens every year. You'd order baby chicks in the spring and the mailman would leave a note in the mailbox saying your order was in. You'd hear those chicks peeping at the Post Office before you got to the door. They'd come in boxes about four feet square and there'd be little breathing holes for them. You'd take them home and put them in the brooder, with a big light bulb to keep them warm and raise them up."

"Ma had more than chickens," said George, taking over again. "She grew most of our vegetables, too. Canned everything from corn to peas, and her home canned peach sauce was the best. For the winter months, we had big bins of potatoes and carrots and squash in the root cellar. Grew our own pumpkins and watermelons. Boy those were the good old days! Say, are you fellows getting hungry?"

Kelly and Maury laughed at him and then Maury picked up the story again. "We used to get cleaned up and go into town on Saturday night. Everyone in the countryside went to town. Cottonwood City was so packed, you could hardly walk the sidewalks. Us kids bought candy and went to the movies with our friends. It was the highlight of the week."

"But what happened?" asked Kelly. "Cottonwood City is deader than a cemetery on Saturday nights."

"Well, I'm not sure I really know," said Maury, his rubbery face wrinkling up even more than usual. "Part of it was the dairy business got more sophisticated. Instead of hauling cream to town, where they made butter, ice cream and cheese, you had to buy fancier milking and cooling equipment. Trucks came and picked up your milk and cream.

"Then too, I think the store owners got tired of working past midnight on Saturday night. And all those kids from those big families started drifting away. They moved to Bismarck or went into the service or away to college and never came back. There just weren't any job opportunities out here. Actually, this part of the country did better because we have the power plants and mines down the road, which started opening up jobs. But for the most part, you could make a better living in Bismarck or Minot, so people left."

The phone rang and George got up to answer it. "Hello. Yep. Yep. Nope. She's not here." Click. "Telemarketers!" he said as he sat down again.

"Tell you what saved Maury and me from leaving. We both wanted to farm because we loved it out here, even if we thought Dad worked us half to death. He was a wise man and he saw change was coming. He talked to us many times about letting go of the past to seize the future. He really couldn't say what was coming down the pike for us, but he knew we needed to think big."

"Dad was a praying man," said Maury, reflectively. "He loved the Lord and he talked to God all the time. If he was on the tractor, you could see his mouth moving. He was having a conversation with the Almighty. I really think that's where his wisdom came from. He insisted that we go into the military and get a taste of life off the farm. Then he paid our way to go to college. George was older, so he left first. He was in the Army two years and then went to Minot State University for two years."

"Yeah, I quit, because I ran into this cute little woman

that I just wanted to marry in the worst way. Poor Bonnie, she'd hardly been on a farm before we got married, but she's done all right."

"She keeps the books and keeps you out of trouble. She's got her hands full!" said Maury. "Actually George probably won't tell you this, but he was in the state legislature for four terms."

"And Maury probably won't say this, but he served in the Marines and finished a degree in agriculture in Fargo. He's been a county commissioner since the foundation of the earth. He's also behind the startup of the canola co-op."

"Yeah, my only downfall was marrying a woman who refused to live out here. Mavis is partial to paved streets and stores. I don't understand why," Maury said. "But fortunately, Bonnie doesn't mind me roaming around here. If the four of us didn't get along so good, we'd never been able to work things out."

"We managed to keep the farm growing and raise families. Did you see the photos over there on the wall of Bonnie and my kids?" George asked. Together they walked over to the line-up of pictures on a hall wall. "That's Billy and that's Steve. They're both in Minneapolis. Annie married a Canadian and lives up there. See here, we have four grandkids, but we have to take a trip any time we want to see them."

Maury picked up the story. "Say, you've met Linda, but later this summer our other two will be home. Janna and her husband live in Washington, D.C. and Tom lives in Washington State. He's got his degree in agriculture and we're hoping he'll move back and start taking over. He and Christy have the two cutest kids you've ever seen. Next to George's grandkids, that is."

The rest of the day the older men gave Kelly a tour of the land, explaining what it takes to plant, raise and harvest a crop. They stopped to play with the miniature horses, which they raised to sell and also to show off in parades and fairs. By the time he went home, after a dinner of steak and potatoes, Kelly's mind was reeling. New information about futures, commodities, weed killers, fertilizer and other farm language threatened to overload his brain. This knowledge was at the heart of his congregations' daily lives.

Once home, Kelly sat out on the swing on the east porch and thought about the day. "Lord those are some wise, hard-working men. I can't believe you sent me to minister to them. I'm beginning to think you sent me out here just so they could train me. Help me to learn all I need to know. And Lord, with you all things are possible. I pray you will do the impossible and minister to them and to the others in these congregations through me. Amen."

Chapter 6

The boat rocked gently on the waters of Lake Audubon as it traveled toward Tiny's favorite fishing spot. It was Kelly's first time out in the boat that a previous pastor had left at the parsonage. Tiny maneuvered the boat like a pro and Kelly was glad his friend had experience, because he himself had never driven a boat before. Just getting it hitched to the back of the pickup and then backing down the boat ramp to the water was a new experience. In fact, Kelly had to admit that the Southern California Kid, as some of his congregation called him, had never gone fishing anywhere but at a fish farm. Ocean-caught seafood was abundant as he grew up and no one he knew went freshwater fishing.

Tiny shut down the motor and picked up his fishing rod. Feeling around in the minnow bucket, he caught a minnow and skillfully put it on the hook.

"Ouch! Doesn't that hurt?"

"Naa. I've never stuck myself yet with a hook," replied Tiny.

"No. I mean, doesn't it hurt the minnow?"

"The minnow?" The look on Tiny's face said he'd never once considered a minnow's feelings. "Nah. See, you put the hook right through the hole between its mouth and gill. It doesn't feel a thing. At least it doesn't feel anything until our big catch of the night comes along and gobbles him up." Tiny cast his line far out into the lake and turned to see if Kelly was doing the same.

Not wanting to look too inexperienced, Kelly tugged on the bill of his new "Your Friendly Co-op" cap and grabbed the fishing rod Tiny brought along for him. He unwound the hook from the pole, drawing blood when the hook caught in his finger. Tiny snorted. Using his other hand he fished in the minnow bucket, trying to catch some bait. The little fishes swam effortlessly through his fingers.

Finally Tiny said, "Ah, why don't you let me do that." He baited the hook in a matter of seconds and gave the rod back to Kelly, who was wrapping his bloody finger in a piece of tissue. Kelly took the rod and, trying to look like a pro, twisted his wrist back and then forward, releasing the brake on the reel. The line dropped straight down, plopping into the water right next to the boat. Tiny snorted again.

"You weren't kidding when you said you hadn't been fishing before, were you?"

Kelly reeled the line in and tried casting again. This time the bobbin landed about 10 feet from the boat.

"Good job," said Tiny, as he reached for the cooler he'd brought along. He dug in it and pulled out a can of pop for each of them. Then he handed Kelly a sandwich and set out several bags of chips and cookies.

Kelly thanked him for the sandwich before he unwrapped it and took a bite.

"What, what is this?" he stammered, his mouth full.

"A brown sugar sandwich," said Tiny, with a shrug of his huge shoulders.

"A brown sugar sandwich." Kelly repeated, his eyebrows raised. He couldn't hide his incredulity. He'd had a lot of strange combinations between two slices of bread, but this was a first.

"Yep. I grew up on them," said Tiny as he dug into a bag of chips. "Ain't this a pretty part of the lake?"

Kelly looked around. "Like a picture. Man, I couldn't believe all the wildlife we saw when we got off the highway. That turtle crossing the road and that other thing that disappeared when we drove up."

"That was a muskrat. Do you see what's over there?" Kelly squinted against the sun and saw a family of ducks near the reeds by the shore of the lake.

"That's why I like fishin' here instead of on Lake Saka-kawea. Sakakawea's too big. You don't see as much wild-life. Besides, it's easy to get swamped in a small boat like this when you're over there." Tiny finished off the chips and took out another can of pop and sandwich.

"More for you?"

"No thanks. I think I'm going to try casting awhile and see if I can improve my distance." Kelly worked on his form as the warm, late afternoon turned to evening.

"Hey, I've got a bite!" Tiny set down a bag of cookies, grabbed his rod and slowly reeled in his catch. "Look at that, it's a walleye!" he said, scooping a fish out of the water with a net. The fish flopped around in the bottom of the boat as Tiny judged its size.

"This here is a keeper!" he said. Taking out a string-er, he pulled the hook out of the fish's mouth and ran the stringer through its mouth and gill. He dropped the fish back in the water and tied the stringer to a hook on the side of the boat. "Hey, hey, we're going to have fish for supper tonight."

"For supper?" asked Kelly, who had that bloated, ate-too-much feeling already.

"You bet. When we get out to your place, I'll show you how to make the best fish you ever had!"

It wasn't until they were back at the parsonage, set-tled into the chairs on the front porch after devouring the best pan-fried fish Kelly had ever eaten, that their conver-sation got personal.

"Tiny, you're a good friend. You know there aren't too many men that would take the time to teach a guy new things. I know I must seem like a real city slicker to you, but you're pretty nice about helping me and I want you to know I appreciate it."

"Well pastor, I figure you'd do the same if I showed up in L.A. and didn't know how to drive in that 10-lane traffic or how to find a good restaurant."

"So Tiny, tell me what it was like when you were growing up."

"Not much to tell. Dad tried to farm, but he couldn't make ends meet. He only had an 8th grade education, so he couldn't get a good job in town. He just worked odd jobs, little building projects, mowin' lawns, shovelin' snow. Finally he started working at the co-op. By then he'd got mean. You didn't want to cross him. But when the owner retired, Dad had enough experience to take over and keep the place runnin'."

"How long ago did he die?"

"Four years ago this month. I'd been working there for a few years and the board of directors asked me right away to take over the co-op. Every time I have a new idea they back me, so it's grown."

"Didn't you say your mother lives with you? I don't think I've met her yet."

"Yeah, Ma is kind of a hermit. She had a terrible time when I was born. I was premature. You'd never know that to look at me now, would you? Neighbors took care of me, because she had a nervous breakdown when I was little. She'd be in the hospital for months and when she was home she couldn't do much. Still can't. I don't know why she's that way. Maybe Dad yelled at her too much and she couldn't take it.

"Anyway, she takes care of the house and I bring home the groceries and pay the bills. She hates to leave the mobile home or yard, so I just leave her to her own world."

"Sounds like a pretty rough beginning."

"Yeah, I suppose it was," said Tiny, staring off into the dark distance. "I always got teased at school. The kids said Ma was crazy and they called me Fat Boy. Let's put it this way, I never did have a date for a prom."

"Well it seems to me that you've done pretty well for yourself. Just 32 and running a business, seeing it expand. A guy could do a lot worse."

"Yeah, I suppose," Tiny said with a sigh. "What about you? Just 23 and a pastor."

Kelly looked Tiny in the eyes. "Tiny, the thing that changed my life was my twin brother's murder." Tiny nodded. Kelly had briefly shared his life story with the congregation a few weeks earlier.

"If Kyle hadn't died, I don't know where I'd be. It changed everything for me and my parents. But I do know this: out of the worst thing that ever happened to me, came the best thing that ever happened to me. Kyle had turned to God before he died. I searched it out and finally understood there really is a God and He was calling my name. Without the Lord in my life, I don't think I would have survived Kyle's death. I wanted to throw my life away. When I finally took a step toward God, it was like he ran to me and wouldn't let me go. I just don't think I could have survived without God. He helped me in the darkest time of my life and I decided He has my loyalty forever."

Tiny nodded in the darkness. "When we moved to town, the lady next door offered to take me to Sunday school out at Cottonwood Creek Church. She had a couple kids younger than me, but her husband never went to church, so the four of us would pile in the car every Sunday and drive out to church.

"She could see that I was, well, neglected. In August before school started, she took me with her to Bismarck and we went to rummage sales for one whole Saturday. She got clothes for her kids, but mostly she got me some decent jeans and shirts and a nice jacket. I even came back with a couple pairs of shoes and some underwear. It probably cost her 20 bucks and a day of her time, but I was 13 and it meant the world to me to have some nearly new clothes."

"I asked her one day how come she was so nice to me. You know what she said? She said, 'God told me how much He loves you and that He has a plan for your life. He told me to watch over you for a while.'

"I decided if God had plans for me, I better start paying attention in church. I loved her and I began to really love God at that time. I studied hard and I picked up little jobs here and there. My teachers began to help me. I began to see they were pulling for me. Well, I never did get a prom date, I'm just too fat. But they did elect me treasurer of the senior class. I'm proud that I earned the respect of my teachers and classmates. Then the co-op asked me to be manager. I believe that's what God did for me."

"And Tiny, I believe that's just the beginning of what He's got in store for you."

"Yeah, well if that's true, I'd better get home or I'll never get myself out of bed tomorrow mornin," said Tiny, as he stood up.

"It's been a good evening. Thanks for everything, Tiny."

"You bet. Let's do it again sometime, but, maybe in the meantime you can practice your casting out here in the creek, if you don't mind me saying so."

Kelly clapped Tiny on the back and laughed. "That may your best piece of advice yet today."

When the taillights on Tiny's pickup disappeared, Kelly sat in the swing on the east porch. Mildred materialized and sat on his lap, purring contentedly. Earlier she and the kittens had moved back under the bathroom sink, annoying him, but now she charmed him into forgiving her. She had purred her way into his heart as surely as her kittens had wiggled their way into his life. He'd named them Mugsy, Boston, Denver and Miss Kitty. He'd been peddling free kittens ever since they were born, with no luck.

The conversation with Tiny had opened up painful memories. As he sat in the still night listening to Mildred's purr and the hum of distant crickets, Kelly began to relive his last moments with Kyle.

Only days before they were to graduate from high school, Kelly and Kyle, along with Kyle's girlfriend Brianna, went to a party on the beach. It was similar to dozens of other parties they'd attended throughout high school. A beach, a bonfire, a boom box, a couple dozen teens and a lot of fun. Because they were in a lot of school activities, the twins and most of their friends didn't do much drinking or drugs. Not that they were saints, but in their freshman year several of their friends were kicked off the football team for drinking. After that, they agreed to avoid drinking and drugs. For the most part they'd stuck to the agreement.

The night of the last bonfire was close to the end of school, however, and some of the guys had brought beer. There were some new faces, but that was typical. Kelly, Kyle and Brianna had been off to one end of the group with a few of their closest friends when an argument and a scuffle broke out several yards away.

A kid Kelly had never seen before was waving a gun around and yelling, while others tried to calm him down. His glassy eyes and slurred speech suggested he was on something.

"..nothin' to live for. I'm not even gonna get my diploma. You think I want to go back to that stinkin' school another year?" he said as a couple guys pleaded for him to give up the gun.

Then as he held it to his temple, one of the guys jumped him in an effort to save his life. The gun went off, causing the girls to scream.

A few feet away, Kyle tipped over backwards off the log he'd been sitting on. His arm was around Brianna and she went over with him.

"Bad time for a joke," Kelly said to Kyle.

Then Brianna started screaming and struggled to untangle herself from Kyle.

"He's been shot! He's been shot!" she screamed over and over.

Kelly's heart seemed to stop for a second and then began pounding wildly. He quickly knelt and looked at his brother in the flickering light. Blood was coming out of his ears and nose and part of the top of his head was gone. "Call an ambulance, quick!" he shouted. "Come on, Kyle, you have to live. Don't give up!" he said to Kyle as he whipped off his shirt and tried to stop the bleeding. He tried to find Kyle's heartbeat, but there was none.

Brianna was standing now, shaking and crying and screaming, "God save him! God help him!" Kelly stood up and grabbed her and they began to cry together.

It had seemed like an eternity before the ambulance and police arrived, Kelly remembered. The kid who shot Kyle had left, disappearing into the night with a couple of his buddies. One of their friends, Dave, took charge, flagging down the ambulance when they heard it approach and directing it and the police to the scene. He seemed to have a supernatural calm that night. He'd explained the situation to the police and gave them the name of the kid with the gun. Then he'd given police Kelly and Kyle's parents' names and phone number.

The medics explained that Kyle had died instantly, and they let Kelly and Brianna ride in the ambulance to the morgue with Kyle's body.

After that, Kelly could only remember bits and pieces of the next few days: The faces of his parents when they heard the news. Dozens of people at their home to comfort them. Holding Brianna for hours. Hugging and crying with his parents. Then it was time for the funeral.

The service took place nearby at Faith Christian Church, the church Kyle attended. Friends and neighbors packed the church and it overflowed with teenagers. After the music started, Kelly shuffled to the front row with his parents, his eyes darting back and forth. He didn't want to do this. He wanted to run and never quit running. Instead he sat down next to his mom. His dad, mom and he held each other's hands tightly as Pastor McDougal said the opening prayer. Someone—Kelly couldn't remember who—sang a solo and then Pastor McDougal read Kyle's obituary.

Kyle's obituary. Kelly remembered thinking it was all an ugly nightmare. His brother couldn't be dead. But there he lay in that casket up front. Kelly could see his face, patched up pretty good and so much like his own. It was like seeing himself laid out. He couldn't remember a day when he hadn't been with Kyle. They'd shared a crib and then a room, then toys and friends. How could Kelly still be alive and not Kyle? It seemed they were too close for one of them to die and one to live on. It seemed like they must also share the same soul. Although, Kelly had to admit, they'd had their differences, Kyle's new-found faith, for instance. Kelly just hadn't understood what that was all about.

"Steve, Nancy, Kelly. Brianna, friends, classmates and neighbors," began Pastor McDougal, after he read the obituary. "We are gathered for this occasion to celebrate the joy that Kyle brought to our lives and to formally say goodbye to him, although he will continue to live in our hearts. He also lives in heaven today and because of that we should not grieve as those who have no hope.

"I first met Kyle several months ago. He had his eye

on a girl back then, a girl by the name of Brianna Davis. When she asked him to go to a concert with her, Kyle was a happy young man. It was a Christian concert and the large and enthusiastic crowd impressed Kyle. He liked the rock music and the special effects. You older people might not have shared his enjoyment, but you will agree with me that this concert was a turning point in Kyle's life."

Kelly remembered the concert. Kyle had come home all charged up, carrying a small New Testament and a stack of CDs that he listened to all the time.

"Kyle liked more than the girl he was with and the music that night. He liked the message the band members gave. They talked about living for Jesus and how he had given them real purpose, real peace and real joy. They explained that we can know we have eternal life if we ask Jesus into our hearts. When we do that, Jesus prepares a place for us in heaven. That night Kyle asked Jesus into his heart."

"You too may invite Jesus to come into your life. If you do, I will guarantee he will help you through the coming days. And someday you will see our beloved Kyle again."

Kelly had been surprised that Kyle had done such a thing. Kyle had never said anything about it. Or maybe he had, but Kelly wasn't really listening. Kyle in heaven floating around with the angels. That was really something, Kelly remembered thinking.

Graduation the next week had been a nightmare. He hadn't wanted to attend, hadn't even planned to, until Pastor McDougal had stopped over. "Kelly, there is one thing you can still do for your brother," the 40-something man had said. "Kyle will never have the opportunity to graduate from high school or college. He'll never know what it's like to marry or have children of his own or a thousand other things reserved for adults.

"But you have the opportunity to do all those things,"

he'd continued. "Do them for yourself, don't throw away your life. And do them for Kyle. Seize every opportunity in life. Don't let a drunk kid with a gun destroy you."

The seat next to his remained empty during graduation. It was Kyle's seat. Kelly received both his own and Kyle's diplomas. His parents sat in the back row of the auditorium. There was no graduation party at their house afterwards. Brianna had also graduated. Instead of having a party or an open house, she and her parents had elected to spend a quiet time with Kelly and his parents. It seemed appropriate and comforting to be together.

The authorities charged the boy who killed Kyle with second degree murder. He pleaded guilty and, because he was 18, he went to a minimum security adult prison within a few weeks of the shooting. He hadn't shown any sign of remorse. Kelly never went to see him. At first he harbored so much anger, he couldn't think of it. Later, Kelly chose to forgive him, but by then the fellow had been moved to another prison and Kelly lost track of him.

The porch swing creaked, bringing him back to the present. Mildred stretch and yawned, then she stood up and "kissed" his chin. He ran his hand over her fur, so soft and warm and real that it brought him back to the present.

"Mildred, did you know you were just on a long trip back in time with me?" He scratched her under the chin. "I'm glad you went along and helped me get back here. The past isn't a place I want to visit very often."

Chapter 7

Kelly made his first trip to Bismarck on a Monday, three weeks after arriving in Cottonwood City. He had a long list of things he needed that weren't available in the little town of Cottonwood City. Besides, he was ready for less prairie and more people. His shopping list this day included cat supplies, kitchen gadgets and a cookbook with easy recipes.

Fast food restaurants were at the top of the things he missed the most. He hadn't realized how much he missed drive-through convenience and predictable choices. In the past few weeks he'd made plenty of visits to the Dairy Cone in Cottonwood City, as well as Schaffer's Café. Members of his churches had invited him for meals. However, it had slowly dawned on him that finding food would be a part of his life from now on. He was, after all, a pretty big guy, and he didn't care to subsist on sandwiches.

While in Bismarck, he also planned to visit Ted Schulte, Aunt Kate's elder brother. Neither brother nor sister had ever married and apparently both had remained in Schulteville most of their lives. Kelly wondered if Ted had as much personality as his sister. No matter, he'd promised to visit Ted, who now lived at a Bismarck nursing home.

Before leaving Cottonwood City, he stopped at the co-op to gas up and pick up a donut and coffee for the road. Tiny was alone in the convenience store and looked up from a comic book when Kelly strolled in.

"Dunderweder," he said as though they were continuing an earlier conversation.

"What?"

"Dunderweder. That's German for we're going to get

a thunderstorm."

"How do you know that?"

"Horse sense. Everyone around here knows when it's going to storm."

"How?" asked Kelly, as he poured coffee into his stainless steel cup. Weather forecasts weren't really important in Los Angeles where each day was predictably sunny, warm and smoggy, but out here, everyone seemed to discuss the weather all the time.

"When you get a hot, muggy streak like this, it's bound to break with a storm. There—look," Tiny said, pointing out the large window. "See the flag over at the Post Office? There's a fairly strong east wind. Sure sign of a storm. The stronger the east wind, the worse the storm."

Kelly's eyebrows rose. "Well, I'm on my way to Bismarck, so I'll be watching the weather."

"Yeah well, pray it don't hail. The farmers here can't afford to lose another crop."

"That I will do," said Kelly as he wrote out a check for the gas and breakfast.

Once in Bismarck, he stopped at a Mexican place for lunch, then took care of his errands. It was midafternoon when Kelly drove up to the nursing home in Bismarck. The July air hung heavy with heat and humidity. Like Florida in the far north, thought Kelly. Even though he'd had the air conditioning on in his pickup, his shirt stuck to his back.

He had stopped at the front desk to ask for Mr. Schulte's room number, when he saw a young woman with curly golden hair walk and a large briefcase walk through the lobby. She looks like the girl at the church! It couldn't be her, could it? He politely tried to concentrate on the receptionist's directions to Ted Schulte's room, but his eyes trailed down the hallway where the curly-haired girl had walked. Kelly followed as quickly as he could, hoping to see her. What if it was the same person? Would she remember him? However, she had vanished. He walked down the hall feeling foolish as he peered into room after room. Finally he got to Ted's room and gave up the search.

"Sometimes I feel like I'm in a bad movie," he muttered to himself as he entered the room.

Ted Schulte sat propped in a wheelchair, looking out a large window at the hilltop manicured lawn. In the distance, the smoky blue hills beyond the Missouri River valley completed the perfect picture.

"That's a good view," said Kelly as he introduced himself.

"I never tire of seeing the Missouri River," said the withered man, his voice slightly raspy. Then he turned and held out a shaky left hand. "Please call me Ted. I'm glad to meet you. Wish I'd been at Schulteville when you arrived, but they seem to think I need to be here now. One half of my body works and the other half doesn't. Thank God my brain didn't shut down when I had the stroke.

"How hot is it today?"

"Close to a hundred degrees."

"Dunderweder. When I was a boy we used to head for the creek on days like this. We had a great swimming hole with a rope hung from a cottonwood tree. We'd swing across the water and drop in. Most fun I've ever had in my life." A smile brightened a face with a strong jaw and gaunt, sunken cheeks.

"How's the church going, Pastor Kelly? I talk to Kate and Marge. They try to come in to see me every week, but they don't say much about the church. Except they really like you. Even Kate thinks you are quite a treat."

"Well, sir, it's a nice little congregation."

"How little?"

"Let's see, last Sunday there were five. Six including me."

"That would be Kate, Marge, Wayne, Sadie and her

boy."

"You're right! The Thildahls are at their lake cabin and the two widowed sisters haven't been coming. I guess there are others, but I haven't met them yet."

"Attendance will pick up this fall. You might get 10 on a good Sunday," observed Ted.

"It doesn't matter how many are there, as long as we take time together to worship God. How about you? Do they have services here?"

"Ah, yes. Someone comes in each Sunday to have a church service. They also do morning devotions each day. That's very helpful, because I can't see to read my Bible anymore." The elder man was silent for a moment, his eyes holding a faraway look. "You're going to have to shut it down, you know."

"Excuse me?" asked Kelly.

"Cross Church."

"Oh no, sir. I wouldn't do that. I want to visit the area residents and invite them to join us. I plan to visit every farm after harvest."

"You can work as hard as you want trying to keep the church going. You can struggle and struggle but it's going to be like rolling a rock up a hill—a lot of hard work and not much progress. You'll get a few new people coming, but then they will get distracted or move away."

"But I—."

"I know. You want to lead the church, not shut it down. But look at the facts. If Marge and Wayne weren't there, the roof would have fallen in by now. They give way beyond measure of their time and money to keep that church going. Ten people can't support a church. Besides, the church was built in the horse and buggy days, when people couldn't drive all the way to Cottonwood City to go to church. Today they drive that far for a cup of coffee. Times have changed."

Kelly hung his head, thinking hard about what the old man was saying. It was true, 10 people couldn't support a church and people did drive a long way for less. But Kate—.

Ted seemed to read his thoughts. "The only reason that church is still open is because Kate is so stubborn."

"But what would happen to the building?"

The old man held up his left hand, palm up. "Let God worry about the building. It's been his all these years. He knows the future and he knows our hearts."

"And Kate?"

Ted chuckled. "God can handle Kate, too. I'm not saying close the church next week. I am telling you that when a suitable season comes, have the courage to do it."

The old man continued, "If anyone should want it to stay open, it should be me. The town is named after my grandfather Schulte. Grandpa, Dad and I all served as mayor over the years. Our family donated the land for Cross Church. My grandfather helped raise the timbers for the roof. Most of my family is buried in the little cemetery at the top of the hill outside Schulteville.

I'm 90, you know. Cross Church has been my life. I served as its pastor for 40 years," Ted continued, after clearing his throat. His voice seemed to be fading. "But sometimes you have to let go."

Kelly sat in stunned silence for a moment.

"Sir, I didn't know you pastored the church. I can't believe no one said anything."

"It was a long time ago. It was always a part time position, a labor of love. And the love of my life. The church thrived for a long time. Then people started having smaller families and moving away. Or attending church just wasn't important to them anymore. After I retired, we joined with Cottonwood church. We've had several pastors—they all had good hearts—but they couldn't breathe life back into

Cross Church.

"Sometimes the nicest thing you can do for the elderly is to forget the medicine and surgeons and let them die with some dignity when their time comes. That goes for churches, too." The elderly man remained silent for a few moments. Kelly didn't know what to say, so he bowed his head.

Ted began coughing and Kelly heard the deep rumble in his chest. Not good, he thought, but Ted got control again and seemed to go on as though the episode hadn't happened.

"Now, would you do me the pleasure of reading out of the Good Book for me? I'd particularly like to hear from the gospel of John today."

Kelly read to the Reverend Ted and then they bent their heads in prayer together.

When it was time to leave, Kelly promised to visit the next time he was in Bismarck.

"You're a good man, Pastor Kelly. You have blessed me today," said Ted as Kelly left. Kelly couldn't help feeling that he'd been the one to receive an overwhelming blessing. Ted's character reminded Kelly of the fruits of the spirit listed in Galatians 5. Love, joy, peace, longsuffering, kindness, goodness, faith, gentleness, self control. He wondered if he'd have those same fruits in his life if he spent a lifetime living for God. He had a way to go, but just being in Ted's presence made him want to be a better person.

****

He didn't notice the thunderheads looming to the north until he was out on the highway. The sight of them thrilled Kelly. He'd rarely experienced thunder and lightning. The summer he'd spent at Lake Metigoshe a number of thundershowers had passed through and he found them fascinating.

Still, there was something about this one that made him uneasy. The clouds towered miles high and seemed to constantly change even as they rolled quickly east. Then Kelly noticed a shelf of clouds under the escalating cumulus clouds. This lower group was deep gray in color and slid west as quickly as the ones overhead went east.

"Oh, oh," said Kelly. He looked in the rear view mirror and hits the brakes. Did he really want to drive into the weather or was it better to wait it out? Just then he saw an intersection where he could turn around. Zipping around to the south lane of the highway, he headed back to Bismarck.

After a stop at a fast food joint and some time spent at a building supply center on the edge of town, Kelly headed home again. As he drove north, he had a panoramic view of the contrasting sky. To the east, deep gray clouds still churned. To the west, the sun lit the robin's egg blue sky. He drove about 30 miles before he reached wet pavement and the smell of fresh rain filled the cab of his pickup. Kelly turned off the air conditioning and opened the window. The air was 20 degrees cooler than half an hour ago.

Moments later he came upon a pickup overturned beside the highway. He slowed down and pulled over, but no one was in the pickup. Kelly turned on the radio and learned a tornado had gone through this area. He drove slowly, watching for fallen branches or worse.

Kelly was relieved to arrive at the parsonage. Everything in place, although he'd forgotten Mildred outside and she was perturbed at getting wet and being separated from her kittens for several hours.

As it turned out, the tornado had cut a narrow band across the prairie. No one was hurt and it had done little damage to the local crops.

Kelly had a great deal to ponder as he sat on the east porch that evening. He hadn't anticipated the astounding advice of Reverend Ted Schulte, nor the strength and unpredictability of the weather up here in the Northern Plains. He was beginning to understand in a deeper way that he couldn't trust what he could see, hear and feel. He needed to depend more and more on heavenly guidance to get him through each day.

Chapter 8

Another month passed. Soon Kelly's parents and Brianna would arrive for their visit. He'd stepped up his campaign to find the kittens good homes, even weaving references to them into sermons. He often talked about God giving second chances and he used Mildred as an example. She was lost, hungry, desperate and alone when he took her in. He'd said, "When we're over our heads, in a desperate circumstance, that's when God's power and love shine through as we turn to him. It was well within my power to give that stray cat some food. Compassion compelled me to do so. How much more able is God to help us when we are totally helpless?"

For another Sunday's illustration he talked about his relationship with Mildred and the kittens. "They rub against my legs and purr. They fall asleep on my lap. They come running as soon as I rattle the food bag." The audience chuckled. "They expect me to provide something good for them. I would take care of them no matter what, but their exuberant hope gives me a lot of pleasure," he said, unconsciously running his fingers through his hair. "In that same way, we humans should show exuberance for our provider, Jehovah Jireh.

He was relieved when a couple families had taken Denver and Miss Kitty, but he still needed to find homes for Mugsy and Boston. He could only imagine what his parents might have thought if he had five cats running around the house when they arrived.

For the most part, he expected his guests to spend time at the parsonage. He tried to see his new home through their eyes and doing so helped him keep it neat. He planned to take a couple days off so he could show off the International Peace Gardens and the summer camp at Lake Metigoshe. Perhaps if they saw these places, they'd understand the peace he'd found with God.

Every day he thought of the girl with the curly golden hair. He'd even begun to think of her as the "Golden Girl," although part of him still wondered if she was real. If she not a figment of his imagination, where had she come from and where was she now?

He'd inquired about any people or families in the congregation he may not have met. He'd inquired about any young women who could play piano. To that, Maury pointed out that Mavis was the piano teacher at Cottonwood City and he named the young women Mavis had taught; none of them matched the Golden Girl's description.

He'd asked if anyone knew of a white sport utility vehicle that he thought he'd seen at the church that night. Tiny had snorted that half the vehicles in the county might fit the description. Finally he asked God to bring her back if it was His will, and he got on with the business of pastoring.

Kelly planned to visit every family in the area, whether they attended Cottonwood Church or not. He wanted to understand the community and the rural way of life that was so foreign to him. He set aside one day a week, Tuesdays, to do this. As he dropped by farm after farm, he learned a lot. Every family seemed to have its burdens.

The McLean family was a good example. All red heads, the large family was a likeable bunch, with a strong faith in God. Their financial and medical problems seemed overwhelming to Kelly. Many of their problems stemmed from the fact that Mrs. McLean, Jean, had multiple sclerosis. Glen McLean apologized for not getting to church more, but explained it was difficult for the wheelchair-bound Jean to go anywhere. The reserved Scotsman was reluctant to leave his wife alone any more than was needed.

After their first conversation, Kelly sensed Glen bore an enormous burden and, perhaps, some anger at God. He vowed to visit regularly and he'd been back twice since. One time he took communion with him for Glen and Jean. Another time he'd brought a book by C.S. Lewis, who had suffered tragedy, but never lost his faith. Truth be told, though, Kelly saw Jean McLean as a pillar of strength even as her body failed. He was quite certain her courage and remarkable attitude inspired him more than he could ever inspire her.

****

Kelly was thrilled when September arrived. Brianna and his parents landed in Bismarck on September 8, a perfect, early fall day. While escorting them from the airport, he found himself giving a running tourist guide's monologue similar to the one Maury and Tiny had given him only a few months before. Unlike his own reaction, his guests were unimpressed.

"Where is everyone?" his mother finally asked.

Kelly glanced at his watch. "This is a 5 'o clock traffic jam North Dakota style."

"Everything is so brown," Brianna commented.

"You should have seen it when I got here in June. Everything was emerald green. Now we haven't had rain for quite a while."

"My father's family lived here a long time ago," said his father. Although Kelly and his mother, Nancy, knew the story well, Steve seemed to feel Brianna needed to hear it. "They moved to California in the 1930s during the Depression and Dust Bowl. I still remember my grandmother talking about dust in the sugar bowl and cattle so thin their ribs stuck out."

Kelly sensed a bit of defensiveness rising in his gut and decided to change the subject. "Lake Sakakawea is to our left. It was named after the famous Indian woman who escorted Lewis and Clark. They spent a lot of time in this area," he explained as they crossed the lake.

"I thought her name was Sacajawea," said his mother.

"Well I guess this is the North Dakota pronunciation," Kelly said. "She lived here for a winter and the state kind of claims her.

"Over on this side, about two miles up is the boat dock where I put my boat in the water to go fishing."

"What kind of fish do you catch, Son?" asked his father.

"Walleye mostly. Lake salmon. In fact, while you're here we can go fishing."

No one responded.

"Well, at least I'll cook some walleye for you. It's one of my specialties."

At the house Kelly was proud to see that the ladies from his church had come in and worked some magic. The chicken and rice dinner they'd popped in the oven smelled heavenly. Kelly knew the spinach and orange salad he'd requested was in the fridge. Someone had set out rolls and a homemade peach pie on the counter. Ah, my co-conspirators, he thought.

"My, it smells good in here. Who cooked dinner, Kelly?" asked his mother. In spite of his bravado about grilling fish, she knew he lacked culinary skills.

"The ladies from my church wanted to do something for your visit, so they offered to make the meal tonight. You'll get one other meal here and that's the walleye, which is about the only thing I know how to make," he confessed.

Kelly couldn't help be excited. He loved his house and

he knew the women had gone through it dusting and filling vases with prairie flowers. At first their offers of help embarrassed him, but he now accepted them gladly. He hoped a good first impression would calm any concerns his parents had about his new life. If they had any concerns.

"You can go on into the dining room," he said. His mother and Brianna walked in.

"Huh!" his mother said. He could see their startled faces through the doorway.

Kelly walked into the room just in time to see a couple kittens sitting in the middle of the table nibbling on a bouquet of flowers. Startled, they tried to scramble across the lace tablecloth, but their claws caught in the lace and they took the tablecloth with them over the table edge. Glasses, plates and silverware went crashing to the floor.

"Mugsy! Boston! What are you doing?" Kelly asked as he grabbed up the fat, wiggly, terrified balls of fur. He took them, one in each hand, and dropped them into the garage and shut the door.

"That's why I've never liked cats!" said his mother, as she surveyed the crime scene.

"Oh, it was my fault, really," said Kelly, trying to keep a cheerful face. "I should have put them out in the garage today. Wouldn't you like to see your rooms? You can get settled while I clean up this mess." Kelly grabbed Brianna's suitcases and headed upstairs as his guests followed, peering over the mahogany railing at the disaster below.

"Mom and Dad, you can sleep in my room," Kelly said, trying to distract them. "I'll sleep downstairs on the sofa. I think you'll find this room comfortable." He presented the room proudly, with a sweep of his left arm. The older couple cautiously walked in.

"Looks like a room from another era," commented his mother. "But it's nice to see your grandmother's furniture in use," she said, offering him a faint smile.

Relieved at her pleasure, Kelly turned to Brianna. "Your room is at the end of the hall and you all have to share the bathroom." He opened the door for her. Walking in, Brianna looked around at the hastily assembled guest room. Kelly had attended an auction the week before and bought a bed, dresser and chair for the room. Since the chair was blue, he'd gone to Minot and picked out a blue comforter for the bed. The church women had dressed the room up a bit, with a couple of pictures of angels on the wall and extra pillows on the bed.

"Ah-choo!"

"Bless you!"

"Ah-choo! Ah-choo! Kelly, get that cat out of here. Don't you remember that I'm allergic to cats?"

That's when Kelly spied Mildred curled up in the pillows on the bed. "Mildred, out! You have your own place, remember?" The cat jumped off the bed and ran out of the room, frightened by Kelly's tone and by the stranger.

Kelly sighed. "This isn't how I expected your visit to start," he mumbled.

"That's okay; I have some allergy medicine along. I'm sure I'll be fine."

"You know I tried to get rid of those kittens before you got here, but four kittens is a lot to give away! Especially when everyone already has too many. And now it's getting cooler at night and I hate to see them go live in a barn. They're used to a better life than that."

"Kelly, don't worry about it," Brianna said. "I'm going to hang up some clothes and I'll be downstairs in a few minutes." She looked around for a closet, but there wasn't one. Kelly hurriedly showed her a hook on the back of the door. As Kelly left the room he saw the set of Brianna's jaw and knew she wasn't very impressed with his new life so far.

"Okay," he said, backing out of the room. "Dinner in about 15 minutes," he called as he trotted down the stairs.

In all, the kittens had managed to break two glasses and a plate. The bouquet was history. He counted his blessings as he mopped up the broken glass and water from the flowers. He wasn't sure what to do about the table, but finally decided to take the lace cloth off, wipe the table down and reset it. He was just finishing up when his guests came down the stairs. He started some music, turned on the antique dining room light and brought out the food.

Kelly looked at his mother, father and Brianna after they were seated. This was so much harder than he expected. "Let's ask God's blessing before we begin our meal," he finally said as he bowed his head.

Later that evening, after his parents had turned in for the night, Kelly and Brianna put on jackets and went to sit in the glassed-in south porch. The western sky still held a pink tint. Straight ahead of them, stars began to twinkle.

"In summer, daylight lasts until after 10 at night up here. Then the sun rises about 5 in the morning," said Kelly. "Now each day seems to be remarkably shorter than the last. I guess by December the days will be really short."

"It's so quiet. I don't think I've ever heard so much quiet. How can you stand it?"

"Bri, I came out here partly because I thought God wanted me to be here and partly to find a quiet place. I think it's healing for my soul. Besides, it isn't always this quiet. Some days are really hectic with demands coming from every side and the phone ringing off the wall."

"Well I'm glad you like it here and I wish I could be here for you."

"You are," said Kelly as he squeezed Brianna's hand. "I understand that you have your own life."

"Oh, I do. Our design studio is into this really neat look. The industrial look. Jontel has this wonderful gift with metal. You should see his loft. Everything is white or metal—the whole kitchen area is stainless steel, even the dining room set is metal. His bedroom has all built-in furniture. Even the floor is stark white. To do that he first painted the hardwood floor white. When that didn't seem pure enough, he layered a coat of cement over the floor and painted it white. It's really a cool look."

"It sounds interesting, but not very pleasant to me."

"It isn't supposed to be pleasant, Silly. It helps you cleanse yourself of outside distractions so that your inner creativity is allowed to come out."

"Oh."

"Well, it works, Kelly. Jontel is very successful."

"Maybe you better tell me more about him."

"Well, you already know he's the head of the studio. He's about 40 and has very long hair: Wears it in a pony-tail. His eyes are disconcerting. They seem to look right through you, but he's really a sweetheart."

"Sounds like a bit of an oddball, if you ask me."

"Kelly! In this case, odd is good. He's made a fortune and the design studio can't keep up with the orders coming in. People are gravitating toward the industrial look, although I'd guess you don't have to worry too much about it getting to North Dakota in the near future," she said with a hint at humor.

"Whew! That's a relief!" Kelly teased, as she playfully shoved him. "Seriously, Bri, I'm happy you are happy. You seem more lighthearted."

"I am. Moving out of Southern California was the best decision I've made. Going to college at the school where Kyle and I planned to attend may have been a mistake. I always expected to see him walking around a corner or sitting in the same classroom as me. The wound never healed. Now I finally feel like I'm free to go on with my life."

"How is your spiritual life?"

"About the same," Brianna said, with a shrug of her shoulders. "Actually, I haven't even looked for a church in San Francisco. I feel God is in everything, so why go to one spot to find him?"

"Well, it's true you don't need to go to church to find God, but you do need the fellowship of other Christians. You need to use the Word of God as a guide. You need to connect with God by spending time with him."

Brianna shrugged again. "I just don't have the same kind of faith that you and Kyle found. I've looked and looked, but I just don't see it. Besides, I think there are many paths to God. You have yours and I have mine."

"You're wrong! The only way to God is through Jesus Christ. He's the key. Until you offer Jesus your life and accept his gift of salvation, every other path will lead you to a dead end. You'll be in the dark about spiritual things."

"Well thanks for the sermon, Reverend Jorgenson! I think I better go up to bed."

"Bri, wait! Look!"

They could see streaks of blue light shooting through the sky. Then yellow appeared and, finally, pink. The young couple stood up to see better, then Kelly unlatched the door and they walked outside, awed by the magnificent light show across the heavens. They stood for a long time, faces raised to the brilliant night sky.

"What is it?" whispered Brianna.

"The Northern Lights. But the Bible says the heavens declare the glory of God; the skies proclaim the work of his hands." Kelly said. "He created this vast universe and yet he cares about every sparrow. Don't get too far from the basics of Christianity, Bri."

"I won't, Kelly. I promise I won't," Brianna said, as she snuggled up to Kelly. "Let's not argue while I'm here. We have such a short time together."

Kelly gave her a squeeze as they walked back into

the house. He sensed that this visit was a crossroads in their relationship. Kyle had both held them together and kept them apart. Now the grief that tied them together was loosening. Kelly didn't know what that meant for their relationship, he only prayed God would be with them during this time of decision.

Chapter 9

Early Sunday morning Kelly rolled over and realized this was his big day. His parents had never heard him preach a sermon and he'd prepared for weeks, knowing they were coming to visit. He'd prayed hard about his topic and had practiced as he mowed the yard before they arrived. He'd double checked the music, the bulletin, and the flowers on the altar. He wanted everything perfect. He'd never felt as nervous in front of the good people of Cottonwood Church as he did when he thought about his parents being in the audience.

Kelly grabbed his watch off the coffee table and saw that it was 5:30 a.m. He got up and rolled his bedding in a ball. He tucked it in a corner of the couch where he'd slept. Mildred materialized out of the dim light and he let her outside before he slipped into the shower. By the time his guests came downstairs, Kelly was dressed and had spent quiet time praying and reading through his sermon notes.

His parents were having a second cup of coffee in the breakfast nook when he and Brianna left for Schulteville to give his first sermon of the day. He'd wanted them to come along, but they declined, saying they'd stroll over the footbridge to the service at Cottonwood.

Brianna was looking especially attractive, Kelly thought, as they drove over the dusty roads. She wore a short black dress with a teal blue suit jacket. Her black and teal scarf draped artfully around her neck. The matching black hat reminded Kelly of a large saucer. A matching handbag and very high heels completed the look.

"You look absolutely stunning," Kelly said, admiring

the warm pink hue of her lips.

"Why thank you, Pastor Jorgenson."

"I hope you enjoy the Schulteville church. It's only a handful of people. Uncomplicated, nice people."

"Farmers, all," Brianna chimed. "Be nice to the 'locals,' she said mimicking Kelly's voice.

"Farmers all, but for one eccentric lady."

Brianna cast a curious look in Kelly's direction.

"Forewarned is forearmed," Kelly said. "And I hope you find out how cool these people are."

A smile spread across Brianna's face. "This is an adventure. I love an adventure."

Then Kelly turned serious. "Actually, it may be better that Mom and Dad didn't come with us. I sense they're having a hard time with my going into the ministry and Schulteville might add to any thoughts they've had about my mental health."

"You know they don't say anything to me. All the while we were planning the trip, not a word. I suspect they really are behind you, they just don't understand."

"I hope you're right. I'm praying that they will come to know why my life now revolves around the Lord and doing his will. Sometimes these things just take longer than we want."

Brianna stared ahead at the road, but Kelly noticed her hands twisted the handle on her handbag. Kelly wondered if she was thinking about her own lack of commitment to God. Brianna knew more than his parents did about God. She'd received the same teaching as Kelly and Kyle. His parents hadn't. Brianna had more reason to be a believer, but she still wasn't. Kelly sighed.

"This is a beautiful morning," he said. "It's going to be a beautiful day. You know what? I think we should go fishing this afternoon."

"Fishing?! In a boat? Your boat?"

"Sure!"

"No way."

"All right. How about this—it's plum season. Let's go picking plums."

"Pick plums from trees? Tell me you're kidding?" she said as she looked down at her long, manicured nails.

"Actually, I've been invited to do some plum picking. Wouldn't you like to take some plum jam back to California?"

"Well, maybe."

"Great! And tomorrow we'll head for Lake Metigoshe and the International Peace Gardens. When you see the Turtle Mountains you'll understand why I ended up in North Dakota."

Just then they pulled up to the church in Schulteville. Silently they walked up the sidewalk and into the church. Kelly's heart was a bit lighter than it had been since his parents and Brianna had arrived. He sensed that Brianna was warming to his new life.

"Welcome," said Ed Thildahl, who served as the one usher at the church. Brianna nodded and Kelly shook Ed's hand before escorting Brianna to a seat in the back of the church. Every neck craned to see who the new pastor had brought with him.

As Kelly walked to the front he seemed to take in every detail of the congregation as though seeing them through Brianna's eyes. Sadie Jensen wore the blue sweatshirt she wore every Sunday. Next to her sat her great-grandson, Cole, with his cap on backwards and his jeans full of holes. Kelly admired Sadie for taking Cole in when his parents had abandoned him. Now arthritis crippled her and Cole, age 15, took care of her. Kelly found it amazing that Cole never missed church and never showed any real sign of rebellion considering what he'd been through in his young life. Sadie, you're an amazing blessing to your grandson, he thought.

Ed's wife sat with two widowed ladies. All white-haired, they looked like triplets. Wayne Selby sat in the front row, near Marge, who was at the organ. A few years ago Wayne had to close the bulk oil plant he'd run. Since then, he'd converted the mobile home where they formerly lived into a woodworking shop. He designed furniture and had particularly good success with his oak pulpits. They sold all over the United States. With the money they made caring for Kate Schulte and the woodworking, they seemed to manage. Kelly had spent a couple afternoons at Wayne's shop, immersed in the scent of wood shavings. He thoroughly enjoyed their discussions over well-cooked coffee.

The most outstanding person in the room was by far Aunt Kate Schulte. Garbed in buttercup yellow and black, her ample body and squared shoulders commanded attention. Kelly was ashamed of himself that her outfit reminded him of a school bus. She stared at Brianna until Kelly reached the lectern, distracting her.

"Good morning, everyone. You've noticed that I convinced a most beautiful woman to come with me today. Her name is Brianna Davis. She is here with my parents for a visit. Brianna and I attended high school together. I hope you will greet her after the service."

Then Kelly nodded at Marge, who managed to coax some sound out of the wheezy ancient organ after he announced the first song. "Turn to page 17. This is My Father's World."

They sang, Kelly prayed, they sang another hymn, took the offering, Kelly gave his sermon and they closed with a third hymn. After he gave the benediction, everyone moved to the back to meet Brianna, except Marge and Wayne, who had some business to attend to with Kelly. As soon as possible, he hurried to the back of the sanctuary to rescue Brianna from a risky encounter with Kate Schulte.

He arrived just in time to hear Kate say, "You look like a city slicker. You must make a lot of money to dress like that."

"Now Aunt Kate, take it easy on my friend," Kelly soothed. Kate ignored him.

"Well, are you going to marry him?" Aunt Kate demanded, her head cocked and her eyes boring into Brianna's.

Brianna blinked and stepped back half a step.

"He deserves someone who will take good care of him," she added in a tone that suggested Brianna didn't have the right stuff to take care of Kelly.

"Aunt Kate! You become more incorrigible every day!" said Marge as she rushed to intervene. "That is none of your business."

"He's our pastor. I have a right to know if he's getting married!"

"I think I can ease your mind," said Kelly. "Brianna and I are only friends. We've never discussed marriage."

"Well, for land's sake! Why not? You make the nicest couple."

"Don't get so worked up," said Marge as she propelled Aunt Kate out the door. "Nice to have you here today," she called over her shoulder to Brianna.

Brianna laughed all the way back to Cottonwood Church. She laughed until she had to dab her eyes and repair her make up.

"Your Aunt Kate is a hoot! Is she that outspoken with everyone?"

"As far as I know, she insults everyone equally," Kelly said. "See how much fun you can have living out here on the prairie?" Kelly asked as they turned into the Cottonwood Church yard.

They were just entering the church when Kelly spotted Maury and Mavis pulling in, with Linda in the back seat of the Lincoln. "Oh-oh," he said under his breath.

As they walked up the steps, Kelly wished he could take back the angry exchange he had with Linda. He hadn't seen her since then and certainly never mentioned it to her parents. He smiled and greeted her, but she barely nodded to him. She stared at Brianna, who stood next to him staring back at Linda.

Kelly made introductions, but he couldn't help noticing how opposite Linda and Brianna were. This morning, Brianna, who was tall and thin, looked like a model and the flush of her face from laughter enhanced her beauty. Linda looked much older, although she wasn't. Her shapeless, tan dress and sandals did nothing for her looks and she wore her hair pulled back at her neck in an unbecoming pony tail. The way her lips turned down suggested deep unhappiness. Kelly wondered what kind of pain she felt, what kind of pain she caused her parents. They never spoke of her after that first meeting, although Kelly saw them frequently.

Just as they walked into the church, Kelly's parents arrived. He took a deep breath. Lord, send your Holy Spirit to help me to speak to the hearts gathered here today, including my parents, he prayed silently.

A few minutes later he stood before the congregation. The church was just about full. His eyes surveyed the crowd. His parents sat about half way up the aisle with Brianna. A few rows away sat Maury, Mavis and Linda. He suddenly realized that he knew most of the people now. These weren't strangers, but friends. His congregation. The thought warmed his heart.

"Let us bow our heads for prayer," he said as his eyes swept across the sanctuary. Then he stopped, riveted on a girl with curly golden hair near the back of the room.

He felt time stop and he could feel the blood rushing through his veins. Was it the Golden Girl? He stared at her, but her head was bowed, waiting for him to pray.

After what seemed like a long time, he found his voice, but instead of saying 'Dear God' the word 'Golden' came out of his mouth. Some of the congregation began to peek at him. He cleared his throat and began again.

"Lord, you've brought us this golden morning, a reminder of the golden harvest season we are in..." What was he saying? This wasn't part of his notes. He suppressed the desire to say, "Will the girl in the second to the last row please put her name and phone number in the offering plate?" What if she left before he could find out who she was?

"Lord, this harvest season is a reminder of the great harvest that you desire. A harvest of souls you love." How many times could he say "harvest" in one prayer anyway? This had nothing to do with his sermon.

He forced himself to get a grip and wrapped up the prayer by asking the Lord's blessing on every part of the service. When he sat down during the following song, Kelly found his hands were shaking. Having three remarkable women in the audience, Brianna, Linda and the Golden Girl, had thrown him off completely. And to think he was worried that having his parents in the audience might rattle him.

"Lord," he prayed silently, "help me get back on track!'

Chapter 10

Whenever he had a chance during the service, Kelly studied the girl with the curly blonde hair and decided it really was the "Golden Girl." Of all the days for her to show up at a service, he thought. He desperately hoped he could talk with her before she disappeared again. One thing was certain, she was real and not a figment of his imagination.

Lord, help me focus, he prayed silently. Calmness washed over him and the powerful message of hope seemed to roll out of his heart, in spite of his very human emotions.

When he dismissed the congregation with a final blessing, he had every intention of rushing through the crowd to her, but suddenly a sea of people filled the aisles, making it impossible to move quickly. When he saw her slip out the door, his shoulders sagged in defeat. Would he ever have a chance to meet her again?

Disappointed once again, Kelly made his way to his family. As he walked the short distance to where they stood waiting for him, he decided to get his parents and Brianna out of Cottonwood Creek. They'd skip the fishing and plum picking. They'd pack up their bags and head to one of Kelly's most favored places on earth, the International Peace Gardens.

It was there that he spent his time off when he'd been a camp counselor at Lake Metigoshe. The beauty of hundreds of acres dedicated to peace between two countries, the United States and Canada, soothed the soul. Although not much about North Dakota impressed them, he felt certain that his parents and Brianna would concede the Peace

Gardens were extraordinary.

However, even before he could tell them of the change in plans, George and Bonnie invited the family to dinner, along with Maury, Mavis and Linda. Wary of how Linda and Brianna might get along, Kelly tried to ward off the invitation, but it was no use. Maury had just learned that an old classmate of his, Jim Barnes, served in the military with Kelly's dad. This was news to Kelly.

"It's a small world!" said Maury, slapping Steve Jorgenson on the back. Kelly knew there was no use trying to stop the unfolding events. The Jorgenson party would dine with the Jackson family. Besides, it pleased him that his father was making friends with Maury and George.

His concerns evaporated when they arrived at the Jackson farm. Linda disappeared for a few minutes, then came into the living room, and announced she was leaving.

"Mom and Dad, I'm sorry, but I just got a phone message that I need to get back to campus. One of the professors is having health problems and I will have to fill in for him tomorrow," she said.

Pretty convenient problem, thought Kelly to himself, as he saw Mavis' face fall.

"Can't you at least eat dinner, Linda?" she asked.

"Sorry, this is pretty urgent," she hugged her parents and nodded to everyone else. "Nice to meet you. Sorry I have to run," she said and was out the door.

Kelly secretly breathed in relief. Even Brianna seemed to relax and enjoy the older couples after Linda left.

By the time dinner was over and they'd walked around the farm, it was late in the day.

"Fishing anyone? Plum picking?" asked Kelly, as they drove back to his house, but there were no takers.

"Kelly, I can't think of anything nicer than sitting in your sun room watching the sun go down and the stars come out," said Brianna. She'd all but adopted one of the miniature horses that afternoon, endearing her to the Jackson's.

"Now that's my city girl! Let your hair down and enjoy farm living!" said Kelly.

****

September 10, 2001, Monday morning, brought a chilly dawn accented with a brilliant blue sky. Kelly, his parents and Brianna piled in the pickup and were ready to travel by 7:30 a.m.

Their plans had changed slightly the day before when Steve and Maury got their heads together and decided that a visit to Jim Barnes was in order. It turned out that by taking a different route they could stop by the Barnes home in Cando on their way to the Canadian border. They called Jim, who welcomed the opportunity to see the Jorgensons again.

The trip to Cando took less than three hours and they easily found Jim's brown stucco house tucked under a row of towering trees. Jim's wife had passed away a few years before, but his son, Danny, was home from Chicago for a short visit. After back slapping and introductions all around, Jim invited them all into the kitchen for lunch.

"After Donna passed away, I had three choices, to starve, learn to cook or be taken advantage of by all the widows in town who were eager to cook for me," Jim explained. He laid a plate of cold cuts on the table next to a bowl of potato salad and a steaming pot of fresh corn on the cob. The standard rural fare of white bread, a plate of sliced tomatoes and a dish of cucumber salad rounded out the feast.

"I think I know what you mean," said Kelly and everyone laughed. "The trouble is I don't seem to have any natural talent in the kitchen."

"Pressure can give you a lot of inspire, Kelly!" said Jim. "Or should I say Pastor Jorgenson? I can't believe how many years it's been since I first met you. Danny, you remember that Kelly took your old job at Bible camp up at Lake Metigoshe?" Danny nodded.

"Call me Kelly. Your idea changed my life," said Kelly.

Danny cleared his throat just then and asked Kelly to say grace before they ate. Every head bowed. Looking at the bent heads, Kelly's heart felt overloaded with goodness.

"Father, I am so grateful for each person here and how you've connected our lives over time and distance. Please be with us during this time together....." he paused, an unformed thought pressing at his consciousness. "Father we never know what tomorrow will bring, but we're thankful for what you've brought us today. Thank you for this wonderful food and we ask a special blessing on the chef. Amen."

"Well Kelly, you took a job as a camp counselor and turned it into a life-time ministry," said Danny. "Sometimes I wonder if I shouldn't have done the same."

"Why is that, Danny?" asked Steve. "Your dad tells me you're a high-powered attorney in Chicago. And I might add he seems to gloat about it just a little bit."

Danny smiled. "It's true that I've done well, but there is more to life than making a living. Any career achievement I've made seems empty. The only real fulfilling part of my life in Chicago is being active in my church. We have quite an outreach ministry. But even so, I'm restless to get out of there."

"Danny came to do some job scouting back here in the state," said Jim. "Turns out there are some good openings."

"You'd leave Chicago to come back to Cando?" asked

Brianna, who seemed amazed by the idea.

Danny had already sized Brianna up and had an answer ready for her.

"Well, Brianna, look at it this way—we don't even have traffic lights in Cando and people wave as they pass each other instead of giving each other special finger signals. We have plenty of culture here, too—why the junior class play is already in rehearsal and the high school band plays at every football game. And no matter who my boss is, he isn't going to be buying and selling mega-companies that may eliminate my job for no reason.

"Huh," said Brianna without humor. "I guess I just like the energy of living in a big city. The mix of people and ideas. Less than that would leave me terribly bored."

Just then Jim broke out a rendition of "Home on the Range" that cracked everyone up and settled the tension that had been growing in the room. The rest of the visit revolved around Steve and Jim's Viet Nam war stories. To Kelly it seemed the stories had grown more interesting over the years.

A couple hours later the pickup headed toward the Canadian border. Brianna couldn't help noting that, indeed, almost everyone they passed waved at them. After arriving at the border, they settled into the Cuddly Quilt Bed and Breakfast and Kelly drove the group to the church camp at Lake Metigoshe.

"Hasn't changed much in the past few years," said Kelly as they toured the main dining hall, peeked in the windows of the cabins and strolled down to the water's edge. "Even with hundreds of kids here, this place has a tranquil feel to it."

"This is really beautiful," said Nancy, who had been quiet the whole trip. "It's so nice to see where you live now and places like this where you've been." Kelly knew she was thinking about Kyle and savoring the inside view of

Kelly's life. He put his arm around her shoulder, glad for any small opening she gave him.

"Mom, you want to see my favorite part of the camp?"

"Sure!" Together they walked up the steep path from the lake and then across the center of the camp to an A-frame building.

Opening the door, Kelly said, "This is the chapel. Kids play hard all day and then they come to chapel and it's like God opens up heaven and they all get blessed."

"What do you mean 'they all get blessed?'"

"It's like God touches their hearts. He speaks to their hearts about their past and their future. After the evening services, many of them stay and pray around the altar."

"It is a beautiful room," said Nancy, walking slowly in a circle, her head lifted to the high, wood beam roof. Near the roof, windows let in the bright sun light, while evergreen shadows danced across lower windows.

"I can see where God would favor this place." She walked to the altar area and stared at the floor. "You say kids come up here and pray? How unusual. We didn't pray when I was a child. We were forbidden to pray, in fact. Maybe that's why I never got into the habit," she said with a shrug.

"Mom, I didn't know that. Why were you forbidden to pray?"

"Oh, it's a long story, but when you and Kyle came along, I decided I wasn't going to forbid you to do anything like go to church or praying."

"You did the right thing, Mom," said Kelly as he gave her a hug.

The next day dawned as clear and beautiful as the day before. The tourists had set aside the whole day to spend at the Peace Gardens. Brianna still felt confused about the purpose of the gardens. As the rest ate breakfast, she nursed a steaming cup of coffee and their hosts, Betty and

Paul Anderson, explained a bit of the history.

"We've spent our whole lives helping to promote it in one way or another," said Paul, warming to the topic at hand. "It all started in 1930."

"No, 1929," said Betty. "We weren't actually around yet, but that's the date!"

"Okay, 1929. Manitoba and North Dakota donated land for a garden. It's a sign of peace between two great nations—the United States and Canada," said Paul, getting into a spiel he'd given dozens of times. "As one of the leaders put it, 'The Garden will be developed for God, and the ages, and will make this old and war weary world open its eyes with wonder.'"

"It's grown a lot since then—acres and acres of flowers and walkways and a botany garden that explains many of the plants found in this region," added Betty. "Hundreds of thousands of people visit every year. We're so busy in the summer we just about can't keep up. Once school starts, it slows down during the week. Why, here it is September 11 and you are our only visitors. That's quite a change."

"Well, thanks for the history lesson. It's sure to make our visit more enjoyable," said Steve as he placed his cloth napkin on the table and started to get up. "We'll have some stories to tell you when we come back tonight, I'm sure."

Just then the phone rang and Paul answered it. He seemed alarmed by some news and immediately turned on a small television setting in a corner of the sunny kitchen. Everyone grew solemn as they watched the screen.

A plane had just flown into the side of the World Trade Center in New York. The television showed the picture over and over. People scurried everywhere. Rescue workers rushed into the giant building. Then the unbelievable happened as they sat glued to the horrible scene—a second plane disappeared behind the towers, followed by a tremendous explosion.

Kelly frowned, trying to figure out what he just saw. If not for the explosion, he'd assume a small plane flew very near the tower. The news commentator seemed just as perplexed. The group stayed glue to the television, hardly comprehending what they saw. As the minutes ticked by it became apparent a second plane had flown into the towers. Commentators first speculated that the twin towers incidents were an accident, but within an hour the president announced they were terrorist attacks. Then a plane flew into the Pentagon in Washington, D.C.

Betty went to Paul and put her arm around his waist. Steve hovered over Nancy's chair and Kelly and Brianna held hands under the table as they watched.

"The Peace Gardens," said Paul distantly, "is for God, and the ages, and will make this old and war weary world open its eyes with wonder."

Chapter 11

The group lingered in front of the television in shock, waiting for more news. All of the happy anticipation for a nice day evaporated from Kelly's mind, like a computer screen gone blank.

"It's ironic that we chose this day of all days to visit the Peace Gardens," he finally said, quietly.

"I think we better head back to Kelly's and then back to L.A.," said Steve.

"Nonsense!" said Brianna. "This is an isolated incident thousands of miles from here. I say we go to the Peace Gardens today as planned. We'll stay here tonight as planned and then head over to Red Mike to play some golf tomorrow. As planned."

A television announcer broke into the conversation to announce that an airliner had mysteriously crashed in a field in Pennsylvania.

"This is war! We're being attacked, just like at Pearl Harbor," said Paul.

"Kelly, what should we do?" asked Nancy of her son.

Kelly sat staring at the live scenes from New York for several moments. "This looks pretty serious," he said. "But we've come a long way and there isn't much we can do at this point but pray for those poor people. I think we ought to go to the Peace Gardens as planned today. We can keep an eye on the news. And then, and then I think we should go back to Cottonwood City tonight." Kelly looked at the Andersons.

"Don't worry about your reservations for tonight," Paul said with a wave of his hand.

"Thank you. Thank you for understanding," Kelly said. "It will be late, but I want to go home tonight."

"We certainly understand," said Paul. With that the travelers went to their rooms to pack.

A light frost had nibbled at some of the flowers at the International Peace Gardens, but acres of hardier blooms welcomed the foursome. They spent the morning walking through garden after garden in bright sunlight, under the bluest sky any of them could remember.

"Look at that giant flower clock!" Brianna exclaimed shortly after they arrived. The face of the 18-foot diameter clock was made up of thousands of flowers, while the giant hands kept perfect time.

"How does that fit with your industrial look design?" Kelly teased. Brianna made a face at him and turned away.

"Look over there—huge flags made of flowers—one is the U.S. flag and one is the Canadian Maple Leaf," said Steve, as he seemed to forget the problems of the day.

"These peace poles say 'May Peace Prevail on Earth' in 28 languages," Kelly read aloud at another site. "Japan donated them. Our former enemy..."

They read the granite quotes of famous leaders who eloquently reflected on the topic of peace. They slipped into the International Music Camp to see where budding musicians spent weeks each summer learning to play in harmony with students from all over the world.

"I don't know what I like better, the Bell Tower or the Sunken Gardens," Nancy commented as they entered the snack bar at lunch time. Their spirits were lifted as they walked from one beautiful site to another. The lunch room was dark compared to the brilliant sunlit grounds. As their eyes adjusted, they realized a television was on, blaring the latest news.

Information was slow in coming. They now knew someone had purposely flown two planes into the World

Trade Center. The smoke from the resulting fires left New York City under an ominous, billowing dark sky. A plane had also hit the Pentagon in Washington, but there wasn't much news about it yet. And there had been a strange crash of an airliner in a Pennsylvania field. News commentators speculated about a possible relationship between all the incidents.

The four sat silently taking in the news and eating very little lunch. Afterward they went back into the bright sunlight. The beauty of their surroundings here on the northern border of the United States belied the terror of the day in other parts of the country. They spent a couple hours that afternoon strolling through the botanical gardens, which shows off thousands of plant species native to the area.

"I can't believe this state. It seems so barren, but has so many types of plants," said Nancy as they headed toward the pickup.

"You'd be surprised, Mom. If you walk out into a pasture and really look you can spot half a dozen types of flowers and dozens of other plants. That's one of the things I like about North Dakota—there is so much here, but you have to pay attention to really see it. It isn't splashy like some parts of the country, but it has a quiet beauty."

Everyone was quiet as they climbed back in the pickup late in the afternoon for the drive back to Cottonwood Creek.

"Speaking of paying attention, look at that!" said Brianna. They were out of the Turtle Mountains now, driving west across the northern tier of the state. On both sides of the road stood crops of sunflowers, their wide heads all facing toward the east. "Did we pass these before? I don't remember seeing them."

"Yeah, we've passed a few fields, but you don't get the full effect until you drive toward sunflowers and you see all of the big yellow flowers facing one direction. Aren't they amazing?" They drove for miles, watching the sunflowers, which because they were facing east, seemed like vast crowds of yellow faces greeting the travelers.

"They are incredible!" Brianna exclaimed. "They're so, so warm and alive! And so many of them!"

"I know a few farmers who grow them. They're native to the U.S. and are getting to be a popular crop. People use them in salads and pies and cookies—I've had them all!"

"Okay, what is that?" Nancy asked. The sunflower fields had suddenly given way to pasture land. She pointed to a piece of equipment out in a golden brown pasture. Kelly happily noted his mother finally seemed relaxed.

"That is an oil rig."

"Well, that's what I thought, but who would expect to find them up here?"

"Actually the state can produce quite a bit of oil, but the prices are so low that it's a risky way to make a living. They say there is a lot of untapped oil under the western part of the state."

As they turned south toward Minot, Kelly couldn't help but look longingly west. The Red Mike Links of North Dakota golf course had his interest ever since he moved here. "Well Dad, I had high hopes of beating you on one of the top golf courses in the United States, but that will have to wait until your next trip out here."

"Hey, remember your mom and I were going to play too, and we probably would beat both of you!" said Brianna.

"Right! Beat us by being first to drop a ball right into the Missouri River. Next time, Bri, you're on."

After having dinner in Minot, the group arrived back at the parsonage about 9 p.m. Sunset had arrived and painted the western sky in a wild purple and orange abstract.

"Just another ho-hum Dakota sunset, I guess," Nancy said to tease Kelly as they climbed out of the pickup and hauled their luggage out of the back.

"Phone's ringing," said Kelly as he skipped up the steps into the house.

"Hello, this is Pastor Kelly."

"Oh Pastor, I'm so glad to finally reach you." Kelly recognized Marge Selby's voice.

"Marge, is something wrong? Besides the terrorist attack, I mean?"

"Yes, I'm afraid so. Ted Schulte died this morning."

"Oh, I'm so sorry. And surprised."

"The nursing home staff said he'd been watching the news and was terribly upset by what he saw. Later, when they went to check on him, they found he had died in bed."

"Died of a broken heart!" Kelly heard in the background.

"Is that Aunt Kate? How is she taking this?"

"Well, this is tough for her—Ted was her only brother and her closest friend, but she's being very brave. I called you to talk about making funeral arrangements. His body will be brought to Cottonwood City tomorrow afternoon and I went ahead and made an appointment with the funeral director, hoping you would be available."

"Marge, I'm sorry I wasn't here today, but I will definitely be available tomorrow for the appointment. In fact, I think I better come over right now and spend some time with Kate."

"No, that won't be necessary," said Marge. "She's about ready for bed."

"Well, tell her I will be praying for her and I will see you tomorrow."

Kelly hung up the phone and leaned against the wall. He'd never officiated at a funeral before. He studied the ceiling as he thought about what a great man Ted Schulte had been. Sadness flooded him. He had enjoyed spending time with the old man and hoped to have plenty of time to draw from his wisdom. Now he must settle for the little time they had shared.

Mildred emerged from some hidden spot and wrapped herself around his legs. Kelly picked her up and stroked her fur.

"Well, Mildred, it's been a disaster of a day. You probably don't know about all of the human tragedy taking place in New York and Washington, D.C., but it's pretty bad. And now a good friend of mine has died. I bet you came to comfort me, didn't you?"

Meow.

"That's what I thought. You're a wonderful roommate, Mildred, even if your kittens aren't."

Meow. Meow. Meow.

"What? You mean you want to comfort me, but not on an empty stomach—is that right?" Kelly asked. He had stocked plenty of food and water in the garage for Mildred and the kittens, but he suspected the little family had pigged out the first day and had to fast today.

He filled their dishes and left them eating appreciatively. He found his own family gathered in the sun porch to watch a harvest moon come over the eastern horizon.

"Bad news, Son?" asked Steve.

"A member of the Schulteville church passed away today. An elderly man who has been in a nursing home in Bismarck. Actually, the town is named after his family and he pastored the church there for many years. It'll be the first funeral I've performed."

At the mention of the word "funeral" the foursome grew thoughtful, as though a giant vacuum had just sucked them back to Kyle's funeral. The shock, the tears, the denial that Kyle was dead all came back quickly and much too vividly. Several minutes of silence went by.

Brianna had tears in her eyes. "Kelly, how can you ever perform a funeral and not think of Kyle? I'd absolutely lose it. I haven't even been to a funeral since then."

"This will be different from Kyle's funeral," Kelly finally said. "Ted led a full, long life. There really isn't a comparison. In fact, I feel pretty honored to be asked—I'm just this pup starting out and they asked me to do the service." He was silent for a few more moments. His parents never talked about Kyle. Kelly wondered what they were thinking.

"What happened today in New York and Washington—that's more like what we went through with Kyle," Kelly said quietly. "Kyle's death and terrorist attacks today were both the senseless killing of innocent people."

"I hadn't thought of that. All of those people must be going through what we went through. Asking why and hoping they'll wake up and it won't be true," Steve pondered aloud.

Steve stood up suddenly, took Nancy's hand, and pulled her to her feet. "Death is a part of life," he said, his voice hard. "You can't dwell on it. Now I think it's time we all turn in for the night." With that the older couple went to their room. Kelly and Brianna looked at each other.

"I don't understand your parents," she whispered.

Kelly shook his head. "I don't either, but I wonder if they have really dealt with their grief. If they haven't, some day they will have to deal with Kyle's death. The longer it takes, the harder it's going to be."

The next morning Kelly awoke to the sound of footsteps going back and forth upstairs. A few minutes later his father came down the stairs and stood over the couch where Kelly still lay.

"We're leaving today instead of Saturday. With all this terrorist activity and stuff, I want to be home."

"But Dad, Saturday is only three days away...and this

is too busy a day for me to take you to Bismarck to catch the plane. Plus, I haven't seen you for a long time and I don't know when we'll be together again."

"My mind is made up. Now I need to call the airlines and change the reservations," said Steve as he strode to Kelly's desk.

Nancy and Brianna had come downstairs and were in the kitchen making coffee, so Kelly went out to talk to them.

"This is crazy. I don't want you to go yet."

"Your father has made up his mind and I think it's a good decision," said Nancy, as Brianna rolled her eyes and shrugged in the background. Just then they heard Steve utter an oath and slam the phone receiver down hard.

Steve appeared red faced in the kitchen.

"Airlines aren't flying! Can you believe that? We can't even leave. Maybe we should rent a car!" he said as he paced back and forth.

"Right! You going to rent one in Cottonwood City, Pops?" Kelly chortled as he headed toward the bathroom and a shower. Because Steve hadn't mentioned leaving early the day before, Kelly wondered if his father's desire to leave had as much to do with the upcoming funeral as it did with the terrorist attacks. It suddenly seemed like death was closing in on them, forcing them to think about it.

Kelly breathed a prayer. "Lord, I have a little crisis here. I understand there is a bigger crisis in New York and Washington, but I also know you care very much for Dad. I pray you will use this opportunity to show yourself to him. And lead me to say and do the right things. In Jesus' holy name, amen."

After showering Kelly went in his bedroom, which had been turned into the main guest room. He needed to get some clothes out of the closet. That's when he noticed a bag full of pill bottles setting on the dresser. Who was taking all those pills? Was one of his parents sick?

He picked up one of the bottles and recognized the name of a well-known anti-depressant and another for anxiety. There seemed to be pills of every shape and color. Ten different kinds in all. Although he wasn't sure what all of them were, he knew a problem when he saw one.

The prescriptions were in his mother's name. Is Mom addicted to prescription drugs, he wondered. Is that how she manages to stay so calm and remote no matter what happens? Is that why she took Kyle's death so well and why she didn't put up a fight when I wanted to move clear across the United States?

He sat down on the bed, stunned. It all made sense now. "Lord, now we have an even bigger problem. I don't know what to do. For now I commit it to your care and ask that you work in Mom's life to free her from these drugs and help her live a real life. Real life is so much better than a pretend life, even if it has some pain."

Later that morning, Kelly slipped out of the house and walked across the little footbridge to the church. His father's plan to rent a car and drive back to California seemed foiled for the time being, but the issues in their lives weren't on hold.

Kelly bounded down the steps into the church basement. In the kitchen he pulled out a slip of paper and dialed Wallace McDougal's number in California. He hadn't talked to his mentor in a while, but the older man recognized Kelly's voice right away. After exchanging news and discussing the terrorist attack, Kelly opened up about the unfolding drama in his family. He told about Ted Schulte's death, how his father was acting and the discovery of the prescription drugs. He wondered out loud whether his parents had ever finished grieving over Kyle's death and whether current events were ripping their wounds open.

"I agree with your assessment. Your parents are such good people, but they have never dealt with Kyle's death. I still talk to them occasionally, and they will not mention his name. They show every sign of denying his death. They've been in this stage of grief a long time."

"What do you think I should do?"

"Our Lord weeps with every tragedy we face. He longs to comfort us in our desperate times, but He wants more than that. If we turn to him every day, He will sustain us and be a friend through the good and the bad.

"Too often we need a wakeup call to turn our hearts to the God of all comfort. That's where your parents are at. I know God can use you to help with the healing process. The timing on these events is interesting, isn't it? He can use these circumstances to help your parents begin to heal. Perhaps he wants to move them on to accepting what has happened. Your father may have "displaced" anger toward the airlines. He's really mad about his son's death, but he's taking it out on the airlines many years later. It may be a sign that he's moving from denial to anger."

"But do I confront them? Do I just leave things alone and see what happens?"

"Pray, Kelly, and I will pray with you. And don't play their games of denial. They need to face reality."

After hanging up, Kelly took Pastor McDougal's advice and spent time in the sanctuary praying until he sensed a peace about the situation, even though nothing had changed yet.

That afternoon, he left his guests to entertain themselves while he went to the funeral home to meet with Kate Schulte and the Selbys to make arrangements. Cantankerous Kate was quietly accepting of her brother's death, Kelly observed. They scheduled the service for Friday, the day before his parents hoped to leave.

That evening after dinner Kelly found his father sitting alone in the sun porch. He noticed Steve sat stiffly in the wicker rocker; his knuckles white where he clenched the arms of the chair. He looked a lot like a person about to erupt, something Kelly couldn't ever remember his father doing.

Kelly felt an adrenaline rush of anticipation of what might happen.

"Kelly, maybe you can tell me something, since you're such a theologian. If God is so great, how come he let all those people die yesterday, huh? Doesn't he have the power to stop things like that? Huh? He just let those idiots kill innocent people who were minding their own business? Come on Kelly—give me an answer!"

Kelly opened his mouth to defend his God, when a thought occurred to him. "I'll tell you that, Dad, if you will answer something else first. Where are all those people who died? Did they go to heaven? Hell? Or is there even life after death?"

Obviously he'd caught his father off guard, for the older man's eyes widened for a moment and the chair began rocking furiously.

"What kind of stupid question is that? Don't side step me, Kelly. I want to know if God is so wonderful and knows everything and can do anything, why he didn't stop those creeps who caused so much death and grief?" Tension filled the tiny room. "Tell me! If you can!"

Kelly gulped, but calmly stated the beliefs that helped him through his own grief and in facing life in general. "God gave us free wills. We can do what we want. We can follow him or go our own way. The tragedy yesterday was the result of men going their own way."

His father stood up suddenly, sending the chair back against the wall. "You're avoiding my question. Why doesn't God protect innocent people from stupid idiots or does he even exist?" With that he stormed into the house and up the stairs.

The next day Kelly had meetings in the morning, then stole away for a few hours with his parents and Brianna.

They drove for several miles, before stopping at Garrison Dam, the fifth largest earthen dam in the world. The height and two-mile length of the dam impressed all of them. Kelly tried to persuade them to take the underground tour. "Think of the insight and sense of space and power it will lend to your work!" he teased Briana. "This is at the heart of what the 'industrial look' is all about."

Later they toured one of the towering power plants, where they gamely rode the elevator to the 20th floor and looked through a grate catwalk to the ground below.

"Kelly, you tricked me or I never would have come up here!" Brianna exclaimed, but she was smiling.

Throughout the afternoon, Brianna and Nancy were in a lighter mood, sitting in the back seat of the pickup cab giggling, but his father wasn't having such a good time, Kelly observed. Steve seemed too lost in thought to care much about the tour. Kelly wondered what was going on in his father's mind. He didn't dare ask.

Chapter 12

That night after the others retired to the second floor, Kelly sat down at his desk and stared at the photo of Kyle and him. Instead of a happy visit with his parents and Brianna, the week had become pretty stressful. Their preconceived ideas about North Dakota had irritated him on the first day. If only that was the only thing that hadn't gone according to his hopes.

Authorities were still piecing together what happened on September 11, but they now knew terrorists had used four airplanes to attack the United States. Two destroyed the twin towers of the World Trade Center in New York, one hit the Pentagon, and a fourth, Flight 93 from Newark to San Francisco, had mysteriously crashed in a field in Pennsylvania. Details were still unfolding, but thousands of people had died and there was hardly anything else on the news.

Then Ted Schulte's death seemed to set off his father's unusual outburst. He'd wanted to escape and Kelly understood why. The terror of September 11 brought back the shock and pain of Kyle's death and made him feel like he was reliving it. His father must feel the same way. The funeral scheduled right here at the church brought back memories of planning Kyle's funeral. Steve wanted to leave Cottonwood Creek, not realizing that he could never escape from the fact of his son's death. Except, Kelly thought, if you blotted out your pain with prescription drugs like his mother apparently was doing.

He'd had no idea how complex funerals were. Since Cross Church was so small and Ted was so well known, they decided to move the service to Cottonwood Church to accommodate more people. They prepared every part of the service so it would bless those who came to honor Ted Schulte. Tomorrow he'd be center stage, expected to guide the process capably. Music, message, meal, Kelly thought. If I can break it down to three easy steps, maybe it will not seem so difficult. The music was all under control. Marge insisted on playing the organ even though she was among the mourners.

"It's my last gift to Ted," she said in her simple and straightforward way. Also, Cole Jensen was singing a solo during the service and singing a final hymn a cappella at the graveside. Ted had spent many hours with Cole, taking him fishing, to ball games and, in general, taking a grand-fatherly interest in the boy.

Kelly had prepared his message, but still needed to go over the notes a couple more times.

The meal was the easiest part. Kelly simply called the head of the ladies aid and let her take it from there. He wouldn't think of getting in the way of those wonderful women and their cooking skills.

Kelly felt a soft breeze before he felt Mildred brushing up against him. He lifted his eyes and she stood staring straight at him. Then she kissed his chin.

"How did you get in here?" he asked, rubbing his chin. "I remember putting you in the garage and firmly closing the door." He looked around, but the kittens were nowhere in sight.

"Well Mildred, you are welcome company and a great friend in a world gone crazy." She began to purr and lean against him, coaxing him to pet her.

"Okay, I'll pet you and you help me go over these notes and begin thinking about Sunday's sermon."

The next morning Brianna arrived in the kitchen wearing a smart black suit. Kelly raised his eyebrows in question.

"I think we should all go to the funeral and support Kelly," she announced. Nancy immediately begged off, saying she had a headache. Steve glowered at her and then turned away. Kelly knew that every time he'd left the house, Steve got on the phone and tried to change the plane reservations. Air traffic had been grounded for days, so he'd had no luck so far and there was still a question if they could leave on Saturday.

Brianna shrugged. "Well I'm going to attend the funeral and smile at Kelly whenever he looks up!"

"Hey, you're a true friend!" said Kelly. "I'll take any support I can get. And besides, you haven't really eaten until the ladies aid has served you a meal."

Brianna wrinkled her nose. "Last thing on my priority list. You're first."

"Boy, you really know how to make someone's day!" said Kelly, marveling at how Brianna had warmed up throughout the week.

That afternoon, long after Kelly and Brianna left for the church, the bright sunshine drew Steve to sit on the front steps. He'd been troubled all week and knew he'd been grumpy, well more than grumpy. Sitting on the steps he realized what he felt was livid rage against the terrorists and the airlines. He was angry at this old man who had died right in the middle of their vacation and he was especially angry with his son and his smug question about what happened when people died.

Too late he realized Ted Schulte's funeral party had moved from the church to the cemetery. Steve could see the whole gathering behind the church, just across the creek. A gentle breeze brought every sound to his ear.

Suddenly a clear, young-sounding voice filled the air.

"Amazing grace how sweet the sound that saved a wretch like me. I once was lost, but now am found, was blind, but now I see. 'Twas grace that taught my heart to fear and grace my fears relieved. How precious did that grace appear the hour I first believed. When we've been there 10,000 years, bright shining as the sun, we've no less days to sing God's praise then when we first began...."

The song reminded Steve of Kyle. The boy sounded like Kyle, who loved to sing when he was young. Oh God, Steve thought, Kyle was only young. He hadn't grown much older than the boy who was now sang. The song's words seemed to enter his heart and pierce it as never before, until he laid his head in his hands. Great sobs wracked his body.

"Kyle, Kyle. My Kyle, my Kyle, my Kyle," he repeated over and over. Finally he took out his wallet and held a photo of Kelly and Kyle taken the Christmas before Kyle's death. Through the watery haze of tears he looked at the 17-year-old boys, not a care in the world on their faces. He glanced over at the funeral party, where Kelly stood a mature man, and then glanced back at the boys in the photo.

Tears sheeted down his face and heaving sobs poured from his body as, for the first time, he fully faced the reality that Kyle had died.

The funeral had been meaningful and uplifting, according to several of the attendees, much to Kelly's relief. After the parking lot began to clear, Brianna went back to the parsonage while he took care of a number of things at the church. A couple hours passed before Kelly came home and changed into casual clothes. He saw a note stating Brianna and his mother had gone into town for groceries. They planned a special dinner for their last evening in North Dakota, since it looked as though they'd be able to fly out the next day.

Kelly looked around for his father and finally discovered him sitting on the front porch holding a photo. "Hey Pops, what's going on?" asked Kelly. His father's face appeared puffed and red, but his shoulders seemed relaxed for the first time in days. Kelly cocked his head at the sight. He'd never seen his father cry, if that is what had happened. His heart melted as he looked into his father's eyes. Quietly he said, "Let's take a walk along the creek. It's peaceful and very pretty."

Steve stood up and the two men headed south along the creek. The water had an uncommon blue color to it and little eddies formed where rocks stood in the water's way. Sunfish glided under the surface, but close enough to the top to flash occasional rainbow colors. The banks were heavy with late summer foliage and the scent of sage permeated the air.

"I've been a fool," said Steve after they'd walked in silence for a few minutes. "I heard that boy sing this afternoon. Something about his voice ripped my heart out. It reminded me...of...Kyle...singing...around....the...house. It really hit me that...Kyle...isn't coming back." Tears rolled from his eyes and he couldn't continue.

Kelly put his arm around his father's shoulders as tears sprang into his own eyes. They stood for a moment crying together and too overwhelmed to speak.

Minutes later, Kelly finally found his voice. "Pops, we needed to talk about this years ago when Kyle died." They began walking again, slowly next to the creek.

"Kelly, your question the other day. Where are all those people who died? It made me angry, but it also made me think. Do you really believe that Kyle is alive in heaven right now?"

Tears again glistened in the older man's eyes.

"I do believe Kyle is alive in heaven, Pops. If we believe in Jesus we shall be saved from death and spend eternity with him. That's what the Bible says. Kyle believed, and so do I, that if you accept God's gift of salvation, you will go to heaven."

"I want to believe in your God. I've been blaming him for Kyle's death instead of asking the question of what happens when you die. Maybe asking the wrong question set me on the wrong road..." his father's voice trailed off.

"You see, to us it seems that Kyle died, but when that bullet hit him, I believe he instantly found himself traveling to heaven escorted by angels. I picture him looking back and saying, 'Hey, I didn't graduate from high school and I didn't marry Bri, but oh well, look what's ahead of me!'"

At that Steve gave a weak smile.

"You suppose he's up there wondering why it's taking me so long to catch on?"

"Probably."

"What do I need to do to make things right with God? There's no way I deserve to go to heaven. I've done some things I'm not proud of. Stuff from when I was a kid, stuff in Viet Nam, stuff since—I've turned my back on God instead of asking for his help."

"Pops, no one is able to lead a perfect life and earn their way to heaven. That's why we need a savior. God gave his only son as a sacrifice for our sins. He really understands what it's like to lose a son. He actually sent his son to die, even though we didn't deserve his gift. He understands the tearing away that happens when you lose someone close to you." Steve's eyes bore into Kelly's in comprehension.

"I get it," Steve whispered. "Did he really do this for me?"

Kelly led his father in a prayer asking for forgiveness and asking God to take the heavy burdens he'd been carrying. Then they prayed for Steve's faith to grow strong.

"So you think the Bible has a lot of answers in it?" Steve asked as they strolled back toward the house. The sun was already getting low in the sky and the birds in the surrounding trees were chirping happily.

"It's got all the answers we need, Pops. I have an extra copy I'll give you. I'll mark out some of the more meaningful parts. For instance, the Psalms have really helped me deal with Kyle's death. If you want to get excited about what Christ can do, the book of Mark is full of miracles. If you want happy, read Philippians."

"Son," Steve said as he stopped and turned to face Kelly. "I can't tell you how proud I am of you. I know I never say it, but I understand..." Here his voice broke again. He looked off toward the west and swallowed a couple times. "...how hard it must have been for you to pick up and go on without Kyle. No brothers were ever closer. When I see you with your congregation here, I'm so proud. You have become a wonderful young man."

"Pops..., I..." Kelly stumbled around for a response.

"Kelly, always remember that I love you and so does your mother. You have fulfilled our dreams for you beyond our wildest hope and with little help from us."

Kelly hung his head, overcome with the praise from his father.

"I love you and Mom, too. You were the best parents—always there, always patient—well almost always patient. You raised us to be responsible and good. I can't thank you enough for giving me a normal, happy home to grow up in."

Back at the house, Nancy took one look at Steve and asked what happened. Steve walked over to her and embraced her. Tears filled his eyes as he said, "Something good. I'll tell you all about it soon."

Nancy looked at Kelly and back at Steve, but before she could say anything, Brianna appeared and started giving orders. "Dinner is almost ready and everyone has a job to do to make this the most sensational meal ever!"

The next day the airlines were flying again and Kelly

took his visitors to the airport in Bismarck. Letting them go was harder than he expected, but he realized this was just one of many goodbyes they'd have to say in the future.

On the way home he mentally began checking off all the personal things that happened during their week-long stay. Anyone seeing him through the pickup window would have wondered at the many expressions that crossed his face—a big smile, near tears, a few words mouthed silently.

He remembered his father waving goodbye at the boarding gate and patting the pocket that held his new Bible. Kelly smiled at the windshield. Then he frowned as he remembered his mother's problem with drugs. He hadn't even been able to approach her about it. Once he'd discovered the drugs he'd easily seen the signs of her dependency. She slept a lot, she had a "whatever" attitude much different than when he and Kyle were growing up. Her coordination seemed off. She had prescriptions from several different doctors. Praying and searching for a way to help her would be a priority. Kelly sensed that unless she overcame her dependency, she could slip away forever.

And Brianna Davis. There was no doubt, their relationship was changing. No longer a school girl, he'd found her uptight and aloof when she first arrived, but she'd finally relaxed. She'd become more like the old Brianna. But nothing magical had happened between them. They seemed tied together—as friends. They knew each other so well it was as though they were brother and sister. And we might have been, Kelly thought, if Kyle had lived. If Bri had married Kyle. They thought alike and worked well together. The day of the funeral was an example. Brianna just knew her support meant a lot. Kelly hadn't said a word to her about it. She even overcame her dread of funerals to be there for him. Yet, nothing romantic had happened between them. Maybe it was time to give up on that spark ever igniting.

Kelly was almost back to Cottonwood City when he noticed a steady stream of cars and pickups leaving the town. As he pulled past the city limits, he saw Tiny locking up the co-op. Kelly pulled into the parking lot.

"Hi Tiny! What's going on?"

"Hi yourself! You're what's going. You've had a busy week. Pretty classy lady you had with you on Sunday," he smirked.

Kelly's shoulders slumped. "I don't suppose it'll help to say again that Brianna is just a friend?"

"Nope. They'll still be talking about your citified girl-friend 10 years from now. If you marry her, well it would be interesting to have someone like her living here. If you don't get hitched, they'll say you lost her."

Kelly stared at Tiny for a full half minute, wondering what "they" would say if the pastor smacked his good friend. Then he sighed and changed the subject.

"I was wondering why the town is being evacuated."

"Oh. Big football game in Garrison tonight. They're our biggest rivals and everyone turns out to support our team. Say, I'm going—why don't you come along?"

"That sounds like fun, Tiny. Thanks for the offer, but I think I'll head home. I've already had a month's worth of fun this week. But maybe next weekend?"

"Sure. And don't be alarmed if you hear a lot of traffic out by your place tonight. A lot of the kids have parties out past the church."

When Tiny said the word "party" the picture of his last high school party, the one where Kyle died, flashed through Kelly's mind and a chill went down his back.

"Do they always party after games?"

"Yep. And they drink beer. Not much else to do around here."

"You know Tiny, that is something I'd really like to change. I'll take you up on that game next weekend and maybe we can talk about what else these kids can do besides drink beer—before someone gets hurt."

"That sounds mighty good, Kelly. I'd like to work with you on that. Seems like every year someone from this area gets in a car wreck because of drinking."

"See you in church."

"You bet!"

Kelly couldn't remember being more bone-weary as he drove away from the co-op. Then as he pulled up to the stop sign, a familiar white vehicle driven by a young woman with blonde, curly hair zoomed by on the highway.

"The Golden Girl!" Kelly said out loud. "She's on her way to the game!" He sat perplexed for a moment. If he went to the game he had a remote chance of meeting her again. He put his blinkers on to turn right and follow her, then changed his mind, and slowly turned left toward home. Tonight even the temptation of meeting his dream girl couldn't keep him from a quiet evening at home.

Chapter 13

Kelly talked to his parents at least once a week after their visit, but he and Brianna couldn't seem to connect. Different work schedules and a two-hour time change didn't help, but the need for each other was fading. She left messages for Kelly and he left messages for her.

Finally, in October a letter from Brianna was hand delivered by the mailman. "Looks important," Tony Schmidt said, a smirk on his face. Even the mailman is a matchmaker, thought Kelly. He took the letter, muttered a thank you and went to the living room to read it.

Dear Kelly:

I'm sitting 10 stories up in my office at my chrome and glass desk. Through the plate glass window I can clearly see the bay. But I don't think there is one blade of grass between here and there. I miss the tall waving grass of Dakota. I don't miss the sunflowers, however. That's because I managed to find a 3 x 4 foot photo of a field of sunflowers. It's hanging on the wall right in front of my desk.

As you can imagine, Jontel is appalled that I would "inject warmth into the industrial decorating movement" that he created. What he doesn't know is that I've decided to make those sunny, funny sunflowers my trademark. Every room or building I design or decorate will have a sunflower somewhere. When Jontel finds out he'll have a fit and threaten to fire me—but he can't because I bring in so much business!

I'm saying all this to thank you for helping me unwind and get a grip. For the first time I'm glad you went to

North Dakota, because you are having a wonderful effect on me. You, Kelly, are most extraordinary and I love you a bunch.

Bri

Kelly held the letter a long time, feeling relieved and happy. In his mind's eye, he could picture the sunflowers popping up in all her work. He was so glad she was, at last, moving on with her life. He hoped she would soon be able to trust God the way he did. It was possible. Anything was possible.

Chapter 14

"This has happened every weekend for the past four weeks," Kelly said to Maury Jackson and another board member, Ken Nelson. The three were standing in Kelly's kitchen, where they had a view clear to the other side of the house. Light, music, laughter and young people filled each room. Maury smiled. Ken pursed his lips.

The two board members had shown up at the parsonage following reports that the new pastor was holding parties after football games. Kelly was glad to have them come in and see what was taking place.

"I didn't know what would happen the first time I asked some of the kids from church to come out after the game for a jam session. Quite a few of the kids are in the school band and play instruments. I thought they might enjoy a chance to get together and make music. I really wanted to offer them an alternative to the beer parties that take place after the games."

"I don't know anything about any beer parties," said Ken, with a scowl.

Kelly ignored his remark and went on with his story. "I asked four or five kids to bring their instruments and come out to jam together and they were excited about it. Tiny supplied pizza and pop. I had several tapes of contemporary Christian music for them to listen to and play along with. They showed up with a couple girlfriends and a couple buddies. We had eight kids here the first Saturday.

"They seemed to have a lot of fun. Lots of joking. What sealed it was one of the girls had a problem and the kids all gathered around and prayed with her before they left. Something transpired at that moment. A bond formed and I knew that we were on to something good."

"So how did it grow to be this big?" Maury shouted over the noise as the guitars riffed, cymbals crashed and someone pounded on a portable keyboard.

"Each week it's grown. We have rules. Tiny or I check everyone that comes. They have to be in high school—not junior high or not graduated. We don't allow any drugs, alcohol or cigarettes. If anyone even looks like trouble, we'll ask them to leave. So far we haven't had any trouble."

"It's a pretty big group for this house," said Maury. "But I have noticed that there are more youth attending church on Sundays."

"It is a big group," said Kelly. "But isn't it nice to see the house so full of life? I'm really excited that these kids are coming out. And you're right, they are attracting more youth to our services."

"Sounds to me like they're more interested in free pizza and yakking it up with their friends," said Ken sourly.

"Kelly, I think we need to bring this up at the board meeting Tuesday. It seems to me you're on to something here, but you'll want the board with you on it," said Maury.

"Yes, of course," said Kelly. "I haven't been trying to hide anything. It all just happened so fast."

"I understand," said Maury. "Well, Ken, we've had our look, let's be on our way."

Ken only grunted as he turned and headed out the door. Shouts, laughter and a thrumming bass drowned out any comments he might have made.

"What was all of that about?" Tiny asked as he came in from the dining room where he'd been dishing out pizza.

"I'm not sure. Apparently someone thinks we're doing something wrong."

"How could anyone think it's wrong for the kids to come to the pastor's house?"

Kelly smiled and shook his head. "Beats me, but it's going before the church board on Tuesday."

Just then Tiny put his fingers to his mouth and issued a shrill whistle, attracting the attention of everyone in the house. The music stopped. "Okay guys, let's get in a circle here."

Everyone moved toward Tiny and Kelly.

"I'm taking a poll," said Tiny. "Do you like to come here after the games?"

"Yes!" they answered collectively.

"Would you like to continue?"

"Yes!"

"Well then, we need to pray for..." Tiny looked at Kelly, unsure what to say.

"I believe that God is doing something really special here," Kelly said, "but in order to continue, we'll need the support of our church board. Let's pray that they'll decide to back our jam sessions and that God will continue to work among us."

Everyone seemed to bow their head at once and several offered plain, heart-felt prayers that encouraged Kelly.

Although Tuesday was only three days away, Kelly felt like it was a lifetime. He couldn't imagine why the board wouldn't support his efforts with the youth, but someone had obviously put in a negative word about the gatherings. He was uneasy about Ken's attitude, also.

When Tuesday evening finally arrived, the meeting agenda seemed to drag on and on. Finally Maury brought up the youth gatherings. After Kelly reported all that had happened, Maury began to speak. He explained he thought the after-game parties were a good place for the teens. He also thanked Kelly for seeing the problem and working toward a solution. He mentioned Kelly's painful experience of losing his brother and how perhaps something good could come out of the tragedy.

"I move that we contribute to the cost of the food and soft drinks at these gatherings. I also move that the gatherings take place in the church basement. That way they can grow larger. It also sends a clear message that these meetings are of a spiritual nature. Also, I think the board should endorse the new teen band that's been playing at church the last couple Sundays."

Someone seconded the motion and the topic opened for discussion.

"I think these youth gatherings are a bunch of baloney," said Ken. "Kids will go anywhere there is free food. We're wasting our time and money on this. We didn't hire Pastor Jorgenson to play with the youth."

"The youth are part of our church as much as anyone, so why shouldn't he spend time with them?" another board member spoke up. Silence followed.

Since there was no further discussion, Maury called for the vote. Maury's motion passed four to one, much to Kelly's relief and gratitude.

After the meeting, he found himself face to face with Ken in the parking lot.

"Ken, I appreciate your concerns and am glad you addressed them at the meeting."

"Well, I'm glad you aren't sore," said Ken. "I'm not against you or the youth. I just don't think we have a problem. Kids will kick up their heels. It's part of growing up."

"So you think drinking is a rite of passage?" asked Kelly.

"Yep. No use in making too much out of it," said Ken. "But there's another thing. Before we moved here we belonged to a church where the pastor had total control of everything. He abused his power. I vowed I wouldn't let that happen again. I didn't like it that you didn't tell the board right away about what you were doing. A red flag went up."

"I'm sorry about that. As I explained, I didn't say anything before the first gathering because I didn't know if anyone would show up. After that it just snowballed. But Ken, you have to understand that I appreciate a strong board, but I also need enough freedom to do what I think God is asking me to do."

"I'm sure we'll get it all worked out," said Ken. He clapped Kelly on the back and then opened the door to his pickup. "The music the kids play at church is pretty good."

Kelly trotted across the footbridge toward the house in the dark, enormously relieved that the meeting had gone well. "Thank you, Jesus!" he said, fully realizing the board had the power to make his ministry stronger or more difficult, and tonight's meeting had been a success. Still, he had a lot of work to do to change the preconceived notion that drinking alcohol was a normal part of teenage life.

At the parsonage, he found a very friendly cat. "Mildred! Are you missing Mugsy and Boston? I bet you are," he said sympathetically. He had finally found good homes for them. Mugsy went home with a girl in the youth group and Boston went to live with a widow in the congregation. He scratched Mildred behind the ears and added, "But personally, I didn't think we'd ever get rid of them. I hope you know all four of your kittens went to good homes. Just think, now you can have a peaceful winter, without them underfoot." Mildred purred loudly and leaned into him.

Chapter 15

Nancy dropped her purse and shopping bags as soon as she got inside the front door. Beads of cold sweat spread across her forehead and her fingers shook as she turned the lock on the door. She moved quickly to the bathroom and opened the bottom drawer on her side of the vanity.

Pink pills or blue ones? Her head felt fuzzy and she couldn't remember which ones she had taken last. Oh why had she forgotten to take the medication along when she knew she would be gone most of the day?

Quickly she opened a bottle and tipped it to shake two candy-colored pills out, but instead the whole bottle seemed to fly out on its own accord. Blue dots bounced on the counter and rolled off the side, landing on the floor, in the wastebasket and rolling under the closet door.

Uttering an oath, Nancy dropped to her knees and began gathering them, dropping two in her mouth and the rest in the bottle. Standing up again, her hand now shaking violently, she swept the pills scattered across the bathroom counter into a drawer. Taking a deep breath and holding onto the wall, she went to the bedroom and lay down.

When she opened her eyes the clock read 5:30 p.m. She stretched and yawned, a feeling of calm encompassing her. Then she remembered Steve would arrive home soon, expecting dinner to be ready.

No more lazing around for Nancy, she thought. Waltzing to the kitchen, she opened the refrigerator door and took out some fresh vegetables and the chicken she had marinating for stir-fry. Before chopping the vegetables, she mixed herself a drink and when Steve arrived home, he found her humming to herself as she prepared dinner.

"Honey, why are all those packages by the door?"

"Packages? Oh! I must have forgotten them in my hurry to prepare dinner," she lied. Quickly she went and scooped them up and hid them in a closet. The house must be neat at all times.

"Shall I mix you a drink, Steve?"

"You know I don't care much for alcohol anymore," he said, grabbing a bottle of water from the fridge.

"I just don't understand you. We used to have such a good time relaxing and talking about the day over a drink."

"We still can. Only I prefer juice or water to alcohol. I don't like that feeling of losing control anymore."

"Losing control? Honey, that's so silly. Do you think I'm out of control?" Nancy asked sweetly.

"No," Steve said and studied her for a moment. He'd just read a magazine article with a warning about mixing prescription drugs and alcohol. Nancy used both, but he didn't know if it was really a problem for her. "I guess not. It's just...I don't know how to explain how different I feel inside. I feel...free. I don't need alcohol to help me unwind anymore," Steve said with a shrug.

"Well, I feel free, free to have a drink when I want to," Nancy said, a bit defensively. "I think it has to do with that church business. Ever since you started going to church every Sunday, you're different."

"Am I? I hope it's different for the good. I've never felt so at peace with myself and with...everything." Steve took her in his arms and kissed her.

"You do seem to have a lighter attitude," Nancy said, a thoughtful sound to her voice. She knew by "everything" Steve meant Kyle's death. Steve had been angry for a long time, stuffing his sadness and pain deep down and then exploding at odd times. Like when they went to visit Kelly and that unfortunate terrorist attack had happened on the

East Coast. He'd been a bear to live with that week.

She was glad he'd found peace. It began the day he and Kelly took a walk along that pleasant little creek, she knew that much, but she couldn't fathom what Kelly might have said to help Steve come to grips with his loss. And going to church certainly had been good for him. As for her? Well most of the time she felt nothing. Kyle had been. He was no more. He'd been a good son. The best you could ask for. She couldn't help that his life was short. She couldn't help that Kelly moved so far away, either. He was a good son, but he felt so remote. Actually all of her feelings seemed remote. It was a very pleasant way to live. Unless she didn't take her pills.

She remembered the packages stuffed in the closest. A little pang of doubt entered her heart. Am I becoming forgetful, she wondered, or is it the prescriptions? Well if I hadn't forgotten my pills it wouldn't have happened, she reasoned.

Thank goodness for good doctors who understood her. Understood she needed help to sleep. Understood, too, that it took more than a couple cups of coffee to wake up in the morning. Of course, the rest of the medication just dealt with that chemical imbalance with which she'd been diagnosed. When she described the hysteria that rose up in her, they understood immediately what she needed to get through the day. Yes, thank goodness for doctors, she thought.

If they didn't know about each other and all the prescriptions she used, what did it hurt? Steve coped just fine and so did she. They just had different ways to do it. Still, she liked the new side of Steve that she was seeing and it made her just a bit envious of him.

Chapter 16

The department store bags had been in his coat closet for weeks. Long underwear, a heavy coat, thick gloves, a hat with earflaps and huge boots. Kelly was ready for a North Dakota winter, but now it was the second week of December with no sign of snow. People kept commenting about the unusually mild weather. He'd changed to a lighter oil in his pickup and asked Tiny about other winterizing. Tiny had installed an engine heater, although the idea of plugging in a car in the winter seemed really odd. Could it get so cold an engine wouldn't start, he wondered? He'd bought an extension cord, a first-class window scraper and a shovel, which all lay in the back of the pickup unused.

"Bring it on!" he dared, looking at the blue sky, where not a cloud appeared. He didn't want to admit it to the locals, but he was looking forward to winter. He wanted to try cross-country skiing and George had already invited him to snowmobile when the white stuff finally arrived.

Kelly thought he'd like that better than duck hunting. Tiny had talked him into that. With a new hunting license and a borrowed gun, he'd set off with his friend. The scenery was sensational—waving golden grass against the blue sky and bluer water—but Kelly wasn't fond of shooting at birds. He was less fond of cleaning and cooking them. Yet, hunting was an important pastime in the region and he was glad for the insight the experience gave him.

Kelly put his pen down and closed the concordance in front of him. Monday was the day he usually began researching for his next sermon, but he couldn't keep his mind on task with the incredible weather outside. That's why when the phone rang, Kelly grabbed it with relief.

"Kelly, this is Danny Barnes. We met in Cando a couple months ago?"

"Danny! It's nice to hear from you. What's up? Are you back in North Dakota?"

"Yes! I joined a law firm in Grand Forks and just moved back about three weeks ago. But that's not why I'm calling. Dad had a heart attack last night and he's in the hospital in Devils Lake. He's asking for you."

"For me?"

"I think he wants to get things in order spiritually, just in case. He took a real liking to you. He thinks you have the answers he needs."

"When do you want me to come?"

"Frankly, as soon as you can. The first day or so is critical and I know he will relax more after he's seen you. For some reason, I can't talk to him about these things."

"I understand. I'll take care of a couple things here and leave after lunch."

"Kelly, I can't thank you enough."

"Tell your dad I'm on my way."

"One last thing, Kelly, the weather may turn nasty, so bring your mittens."

"No kidding? That's what I've been waiting for!"

Kelly called Maury and left a message telling him what had happened, and gathered his winter gear in the pickup, along with an overnight bag. He added extra food to Mildred's bowl. Then he headed for the highway. Kelly prayed for Jim, prayed his health would be restored and about what to say to Jim. He didn't pay much attention to the changing sky. He'd driven 50 miles when the sunny sky filled with deep gray clouds. After another 20 miles it began to snow.

Kelly didn't think he'd ever seen anything as beautiful as those huge snowflakes. The temperature dropped considerably, so he pulled over and put his coat on and turned up the heater.

The amount of snow falling kept increasing, and soon the ground was white. He remembered an old song about a winter wonderland. That's what he saw outside between swipes of the windshield wiper. Devils Lake was still about 30 miles away when a gust of wind hit the pickup causing a low "whoa" to escape Kelly's lips. Within a couple miles, the pickup started sliding as the cold snow hit the warm pavement and turned to ice.

Kelly marveled at how few vehicles he passed on the road, aware that the locals probably knew enough to stay off the road in this weather. Nothing had prepared him for driving in six inches of slush with wind gusting at 30 miles per hour and almost zero visibility. He slowed down to a crawl and hoped for the next town to appear soon.

Instead, a car appeared. Kelly pulled to the side of the road and ran over to the small black sports car, which set at an angle in the ditch. Heaving the door open, he stared at the occupant.

"Linda Jackson?" he shouted, but the howling wind forced the words back in his mouth. He grabbed her arm and helped her climb out of the car. Her standard angry appearance had disappeared and her face now reflected a mixture of fear and relief.

"Can you give me a ride to New Rockford?" she asked, the wind blowing her words in every direction. Kelly wasn't sure he understood her, but nodded for her to come with him. She turned and pulled her purse and overnight bag out of the car.

They scrambled to the pickup, faces and coats wet with snow, gasping for breath that the wind tried to pull from them. Once inside, Kelly turned and studied Linda, seeing something different in her, a vulnerability that hadn't been there in their previous encounters.

"Thanks for stopping. I'd been there about a half hour and not one car came by!" she said. "New Rockford is just up the road about five miles."

"Okay, New Rockford here we come, speeding along like a limping turtle." A glance at Linda's white face told Kelly that she saw no humor in their predicament. He pulled the pickup back out on the road and he realized in the few minutes he'd stopped, the road had gotten worse.

"Where were you coming from?" he asked.

"I drove down to Cottonwood City yesterday afternoon. Didn't have to work today and I hadn't been home for a while," Linda said with a sideways glance at him.

Probably since that miserable Sunday in September, Kelly thought. Her parents hadn't mentioned her since then.

"And you? Where are you headed in this horrible storm?"

"A friend had a heart attack. He's in the hospital at Devils Lake. He wanted me to come. The weather was fine when I left home."

"I'd tell you that you need to check the weather before leaving home up here, but I listened to the news and weather on the radio this morning and still didn't expect this." Linda was silent for a couple minutes and Kelly could have sworn he saw tears in her eyes, not that he could take a good look. It took all of his driving skill to keep the pickup on the icy road and a good deal of squinting to see the road ahead in the blinding snow.

"People die in these storms. Every year. When we get to New Rockford, we'd better get off the road until the storm clears. There's a café on the edge of town." That said, Linda seemed to shrink inside her green Army parka.

The café felt warm and safe to Kelly as they found a booth by a window. Outside the snow swirled like a scene from a movie. Kelly thanked God they'd made it to safety. They ordered coffee, then Kelly asked how long Linda thought the storm might last.

"Could be a few hours or a few days," she said and then was quiet.

Kelly excused himself and went to call Danny. He reported his location and companion.

"You're with Linda Jackson who grew up in Cottonwood City?" Danny asked incredulously.

"That would be the one," said Kelly, curious about Danny's excitement. Did he know Linda?

"Man, I haven't seen her since high school. Our families were friends and we always did things together. Never dated, of course."

"Of course," Kelly repeated, wondering what Linda was like in high school. Danny said his father was in stable condition and encouraged him to stay safe. Kelly promised to head for Devil's Lake as soon as the weather cleared.

Back at the booth, Kelly said to Linda, "I didn't make the connection that you knew Danny Barnes. His father is the person who had a heart attack."

"Jim Barnes had a heart attack? I am sorry to hear that. Our families were friends when I was growing up, but they moved away when I was in high school."

Several hours passed and they ordered hamburgers and fries for dinner. The owner came by to tell them and other stranded travelers they could spend the night if the storm didn't let up.

The street lights were only occasionally visible as the storm howled on. The owner of the café came by about 9 p.m. and suggested they bring in any blankets or warm clothing and use them for bedding. Others stranded at the café would also spend the night. Everyone helped move tables and chairs to the side of the room. Kelly went to claim his survival kit, which included a sleeping bag and small pillow. He insisted Linda use them. He laid them out in the area where the stranded travelers were bedding down and then sat down in the booth again.

Instead of moving to her bed on the floor, Linda stayed huddled in the booth, staring out the window.

"My friend died in a storm like this," she said.

Kelly wasn't sure he heard her correctly. "Did you say a friend died in a storm like this?" He was almost afraid to breathe, as he sensed, hoped, and yet dreaded what Linda might say next.

"Her name was Rachel. She was 15. The story that appeared in the newspaper said she'd left home just as the storm started and wasn't dressed for bad weather. It said she got confused and ended up in the creek instead of in town."

Silence followed and Kelly wondered if she was reliving the tragedy. Finally he said, "Is that the true story or do you know more about it?"

Linda nodded grimly. "Rachel ran out in the storm on purpose." Another silence followed.

"Have you ever felt responsible for someone else's death?" she asked.

"You feel responsible?"

Linda was silent a long time.

Kelly finally gently said, "If you have a story to tell, I seem to have a lot of time to listen. Long moments like this don't happen very often and sometimes they happen for a reason. I promise I won't preach at you or judge you in any way."

Linda smiled grimly as she stirred a spoon around in her cold cup of coffee. When she looked up, pain seemed to overflow from her eyes. She shook her head sadly and began a whispered story.

"Rachel and I always went to her house after school. They lived on a farm just outside of town and they had horses. We'd ride or care for the horses every day. One day we met this guy who had moved into a shack between town and Rachel's place. He started talking to us every afternoon. He'd tease us and he was nice.

"One day he asked us into his house. We weren't going to go at first and then I said I thought we should. He offered us beer. We didn't take any, but we started going to the house every afternoon. It was in the fall and the days were getting cooler. Every day he'd offer us a beer and one day I said yes, so Rachel had some, too.

"Finally one day he said he was falling in love with one of us, but he couldn't figure out which one. He wanted to kiss both of us. I said yes. His kiss was filled with the passion of an adult man. It shook me up. I felt like I'd stepped into a dream world and this really wasn't happening. No, to me it was like waking up in the middle of a nightmare— it scared me. He seemed to think he'd done me a favor by kissing me. Then he wanted to kiss Rachel. She said okay. After he kissed her, he said it was Rachel and he wanted to be alone with her. This was big stuff for us. We'd never been kissed or had real boyfriends.

"It was all very dramatic. If only I would have seen it for what it was: a creep living in a shack, seducing young girls. And truthfully, I was secretly relieved he didn't pick me. When he said he wanted to be alone with Rachel, I left."

Linda buried her head in her hand and tears leaked between her fingers. "I left her alone with him. After that Rachel went alone to his house after school." Linda was silent for several minutes as she struggled to control her feelings. Others in the café were glancing at them, but Kelly was pretty sure they were too far away to overhear the horrible story. Finally Linda continued.

"Some time passed and I, I kept the romance a secret. One day Rachel told me she thought she was going to have a baby. She wasn't even scared, she was happy. That's because she knew this guy loved her and would take care of her. I didn't know what to say. It all seemed surreal, like we were living out a story in a romance magazine. And I still didn't tell anyone."

Linda paused again for some time. Kelly was barely aware of the wind and snow beating against the building. He laid his hand across Linda's arm, trying to comfort her and urge her on.

"Rachel told him she was pregnant that afternoon and the next day he was gone. She didn't know what to do. She waited and cried for a week, thinking he'd be back. Finally she realized he was really gone. Then she got scared. And I still didn't tell my parents or her parents or our teachers or our youth leader, no one. Why? Why didn't I tell anyone?" Linda's eyes darted back and forth as she relived the nightmare.

"I was home doing my homework the night Rachel ran out in the storm. Deep in my heart I know she ran out on purpose, hoping she would never have to tell her parents. I should have known how upset and frightened she was." Linda's voice was flat, with all the emotion squeezed out by years of guarding the truth.

"You've never told anyone?"

She shook her head. "Not even when they fished her body out of the creek."

No wonder Linda seems to hate men, Kelly thought. No wonder she doesn't like storms. They open an old wound and all the pain comes oozing out, just like the events of 9-11 and Ted Schulte's death opened the wound in Dad's heart. "Lord," Kelly prayed silently. "Do a work in Linda's heart, like you did in Dad's."

"Have you ever told anyone this story before?" he asked.

"No."

"Why are you telling me?"

"Dragging this secret around with me is like dragging around a boulder. Only it gets heavier as time passes. I'm... sinking," she said, her voice breaking. Then she picked up the story again. "Then I ran in the ditch in this storm. I wondered if I would die like Rachel," said Linda, her voice growing thin with emotion. "I always felt I deserved to die like her, but sitting in the ditch in a blizzard, I realized I really don't want to die." Tears continued to sheet down her face, and her mouth turned down, her lower lip sticking out.

"Then you stopped. Not one of my goddess friends or college colleagues or a perfect stranger. You. I have blamed God all these years for what happened. I turned my back on him in spite of all my parents' taught me and their example of faith. Then as I sat in that ditch I was desperate. And I said, 'God, if you're real, I need your help. And suddenly you were there."

"Linda, I'm so glad I was at the right place at the right time," Kelly said. He could feel tears in his own eyes and the warmth of gratitude for what was surely God's timing. "And I'm so honored that you trust me enough to tell me. I will keep this in confidence.

"I don't know if you know about my twin brother. But perhaps it would help you to know my twin brother died in front of my eyes. After that I spent a lot of time doing nothing but searching for answers and trying to cope with the pain. I asked myself every day what I could have done to prevent his death." He shook his head, then reached across the table and tilted Linda's downcast face up until her eyes met his. "It was only after I almost destroyed myself that I found peace.

"Linda, you were 15. You weren't responsible. That man was a child predator, a rapist and a con artist. You were never meant to carry this burden."

"I know the guy was a criminal up here," Linda said,

tapping her head. "But I'm the one who said yes to going into his house and to drinking beer and to letting him kiss me. If I hadn't done those things, Rachel probably wouldn't have either. She died so young and missed so much, that I feel I should never be happy. She lost her life because of my foolishness."

"Linda," Kelly said, taking her hands in his. "Forgive yourself."

"I can't," she said loudly enough for the people trying to sleep at the other end of the room to look up. She seemed to grit her teeth and will the tears to stop, but they kept coming.

After a moment Kelly continued. "Think of all the people who lost loved ones on September 11. Don't you think every one of them is saying 'If only....?' We can't live in the past or make it change. We can only make the best of today.

"You've already taken the first step, by opening up. A burden like this can't have power over you unless it's kept a secret. Besides, the best thing you can do for Rachel now is to live the fullest life you can. You can't do that unless you forgive yourself and give yourself permission to go on. See, hear, touch, smell each new day, because it's a gift she wasn't given. That's not my wisdom, it's what a very wise friend made me see."

The tension seemed to drain from Linda's face and shoulders. She sat silently for a few moments. "Suddenly I'm really tired," she said. "Thank you for listening...and understanding." She slipped from the booth and made her way through the dimly lit room to the sleeping bag. Kelly pounded his jacket into a pillow and lay awake a long time thinking about the revelation Linda had made.

Things began to stir in the café long before the first sun beams peeped over the little town. The wind had died down along with the snowfall.

Kelly gazed out the window at the snow-covered land-scape, amazed at the change that took place in less than a day. Then he looked up and Linda stood by the booth. Her eyes were red and Kelly wondered how long she had cried, the sleeping bag muffling the sound. Still, she didn't seem as glum as usual and the tightness around her eyes seemed softened.

"Did you sleep?" asked Kelly.

"It took a while, but then I slept like a baby. Thank you for listening last night. I can't believe I told you the whole thing. It was like I couldn't contain it any more. I'm just glad you were here to talk with."

"I'm glad I could be here, too."

"I still have a lot to think about, but I feel that some-thing changed last night."

"Anytime you want to talk, I'll be happy to listen," said Kelly. "In the meantime, I'll keep praying for you."

The sun came up, revealing a bright, white world out-side the window. News circulated through the café that the roads would be open in a few hours. Kelly and Linda de-vised a plan. Linda would arrange for a tow truck to pull her car from the ditch. Since it likely wouldn't be towed for several hours, she would ride with Kelly to Devils Lake. On the return trip he could drop her off. By then the tow truck should have her car out of the ditch and ready to go. The urgency of getting back to Grand Forks had disappeared because the university had canceled classes so she didn't have to teach that day.

Two hours later they eased onto the highway, grateful that a snowplow had finally cleared the way before them. At Mercy Hospital in Devils Lake, they found Jim Barnes was mending. Kelly pulled up a chair next to the hospital bed for a private talk with Jim. Down in the coffee shop, Danny and Linda visited while they waited. They had a lot to catch up on.

Later that day, Kelly and Linda drove back to New Rockford and Kelly dropped Linda off at the garage. The tow truck had brought in her car, which had received only minor damage, so she left for Grand Forks, while Kelly drove off in the opposite direction.

Back at Cottonwood Creek, Kelly marveled that it was only Tuesday evening. It felt like he'd been gone for a week. He arrived after dark to find his driveway blocked with snow. The yard light cast a blue glow over the largest snow drift he'd ever seen. After pulling on his snowmobile suit, he took the tractor out of the garage and began pushing snow with the scoop that replaced the lawnmower blade. By the time he got into the house, Kelly wanted nothing more than to eat a bowl of soup and go to bed.

Mildred met him at the door and he scooped her up, glad for her warm and happy greeting.

"Madam, you're toasty warm. Wasn't it lucky I left you in the house instead of the garage? I suppose you want to share a meal with me, since you obviously ate all of your food as soon as I drove out of the driveway."

Meow.

"You better be careful, you're looking a little chubby and since our little trip to the vet, I don't think it's because you are in a family way."

Meow. Mildred struggled to get down, so Kelly let her slip to the floor.

There were five phone messages. Two church members and Brianna all called to see how he liked the snow. Jean McLean called to invite him for Christmas dinner. And Kate Schulte wanted to talk about the future of Cross Church.

Chapter 17

Kelly sat like a school boy face to face with Kate Schulte. Someone had placed fragrant evergreen boughs on the coffee table and a small artificial Christmas tree stood in a corner of the living room. Kelly thought Aunt Kate had aged considerably in the six months Kelly had been her pastor. Being well into her 80s and recently losing her only brother no doubt contributed to the sagging jaw line and wrinkled face. What really bothered Kelly though, was the stoop of the once square shoulders. Kate seemed to be giving up, he thought sympathetically.

"Shut the door when you leave and don't come back until I ring the bell," Kate ordered Marge Selby, her friend and caretaker. Okay, thought Kelly, maybe she isn't as frail as she appears.

"Aunt Kate, you shouldn't talk like that in front of Pastor Jorgenson," chided Marge as she closed the door.

Once they were alone in the yellow living room of the finest home in Schulteville, Kate focused her attention on Kelly.

"I've come to a decision about Cross Church," she said as though it were her personal possession.

"When I die, which could be any day," she said, a look of self pity passing over her face, "I want you to combine it with Cottonwood Church. It should be closed right now, but I don't want anyone saying the last thing I did was close down the church that's meant so much to my family. People talk, you know," she said, her dentures clicking.

Kelly's eyebrows shot up and he opened his mouth to respond, but Kate was ready to carry on the conversation quite nicely without him.

"The board won't be any problem. It's just Wayne and Ed Thildahl and me. Ed lives closer to Cottonwood Church than he does to Schulteville. The only problem is those old ladies that live here will need a ride, but they'll die off soon enough."

Kelly waved his hand in an effort to interrupt, but Kate kept rolling.

"For the time being, Wayne can give them a ride in that van of his. That will assuage his feelings of guilt."

Kelly made a sound as if to speak, but Kate ignored him.

"He'll feel guilty, but can you think of a better use for an old church than to turn it into a wood shop where he makes church altars? He needs to get out of that awful trailer before it burns down on him. Of course, he doesn't know any of this yet. You'll have to tell him. When the time comes."

"You're wrong, Aunt Kate." Kelly finally found his voice. He so startled Kate that, even though her mouth was open to speak, she shut it.

"You're a powerful woman with a long history of making good decisions and being a pillar of strength. You wouldn't leave something as sacred as closing the church to some wet-behind the ears preacher, would you?"

Kate stared at him, a flicker of a smile crossing her lips.

"Until you and the rest of the board decide it's time to close Cross Church, I vow to keep it open as long as I serve here. I'll visit every family in the county to find members if need be."

Kate's shoulders sagged a little more and her next words came out in a whine. "What would people think if I closed the church? What would Ted think? He loved the church so."

Kelly suddenly realized something. Something that Kate didn't know about her brother. They might have been best friends, but they still kept secrets from each other.

"It breaks my heart to see it close," said Kate dramatically. "But I have this vision of Wayne, dear Wayne, opening a wonderful shop there. It's such a perfect solution. Maybe he'll call it Cross Church Furniture. I doubt Ted would understand replacing the sacred with a business, even if it glorifies our blessed Lord."

Kelly smiled and took Kate's hand. "Can I tell you about my first conversation with Ted?" Kate nodded, her blue-white curly hair waving with her head.

"He told me how he'd been pastor of Cross Church for 40 years. I didn't know that. My respect for him deepened when I realized all the wisdom he had. I went to see him as often as possible. He was a very wise man and he knew people so well. He was just what I needed as I started out here.

"But he also told me a season would come when Cross Church should be closed. He said he did what he could to keep it open for your sake."

"My Ted said he kept the church open for my sake?" Kate asked incredulously. "I never knew...I tried to keep it open for both of us. Oh we are a pair, aren't we?" she mused, using the present tense as though Ted were still alive.

"Why don't you pray about it some more, Aunt Kate, before bringing the idea to the other board members? I'll abide by whatever decision you make."

"Young man, I'm going to listen to you. And Ted," Kate said. Kelly breathed a sigh of relief, feeling as though he'd just had a small victory.

Kate rose from her yellow wing-backed chair, tottered over to a closet and pulled out her purse. "And dear Pastor Jorgenson, thank you for everything. This is an early Christmas present." She pressed something into his hand. Surprised, he murmured his thanks and shook her hand before hurrying out the door. Once in his pickup, he looked to see what she'd given him. Two crisp $1 bills.

It was Kelly's first Christmas away from home. He couldn't leave his congregation at one of the most holy times of the year to be with his parents and he was grateful they planned to go to his aunt and uncle's home. Free from concern about them being alone for the holiday, he looked forward to his first white Christmas and the first as a pastor. He enjoyed bringing out the Christmas wreaths and candles to decorate the church. He looked forward to helping with the Christmas program, planned for the Sunday evening before Christmas. He also wanted to take special care to make the Christmas Eve service meaningful to everyone who attended.

At the house he'd put up a small tree and let the youth group decorate it. The only thing he added was a photo of Kyle in a little frame, which Brianna had given him years before. The materialism of Christmas had died for him when Kyle was no longer there to share in gift opening.

Chapter 18

Nancy sat in her perfectly decorated living room, the snowy white carpet offset by deep red candles, holly wreaths and deep green swags. The live tree stood next to the fireplace, ablaze in white lights. She liked to change up her Christmas decorations each year and this year was no different—she'd been picking up ideas since October. However, they wouldn't be spending the holiday at the house. They had made plans to visit her brother and his wife.

Good thing, too. Christmas 2001 looked to be the gloomiest ever. Since Kyle's death, they'd scrambled to make the holiday festive and Kelly had always been here to help. Now, for the first time Nancy could see no way to mask over the glaring hole in their lives except to escape to her brother's.

A sigh escaped her. How many years had it been since Kelly and Kyle had livened up Christmas with their antics? She remembered them as small boys, running to the tree in their blue sleepers one long-ago Christmas morning. Their excitement over opening gifts. Their little arms hugging her with big a "thank yew" from each of them. She remembered...

The front door opened and Steve walked in. "Hi Honey! Are you ready for the great escape?"

Nancy meant to answer, but when Steve said the word "escape" it triggered a reaction she never expected. She opened her mouth to speak and all that came out was a desperate cry.

"Nancy! What's wrong?" Steve was on his knees next to her chair in a flash.

Nancy huffed, trying to catch her breath. "I don't know. Oh Steve, I do know. I can't bear it that Kyle died. I can't bear it that Kelly is so far away." She put her arms around his neck and hung on as though she feared he'd disappear, too. "It hurts so bad. Oh Steve, do you know I've been burying my grief with medication? The last few weeks I decided to take less and less, but now I feel so much more...of everything. Pain because Kyle's gone. And more love for Kelly and for you, Steve. I love you so much."

Words continued to gush from Nancy as long-buried pain began to surface.

"Nancy, tell me about the medication!"

"I've been using prescription meds, too many of them. And drinking. I'm not stupid. I know better, but all these years I've depended on the drugs to help me cope. They make me do things I'm ashamed of."

Steve started to protest, but she held up a hand. "Let me finish, while I have the courage to do so. I've lied to you. Lied to doctors. Crawled around on the floor picking up pills when I shook too much to hold onto a bottle. I knew it was wrong, but I was desperate to escape the pain..."

Steve tried to take in all his wife of 27 years was saying. He'd known she took various kinds of medication, but he'd never questioned her about it. He'd heard of people being addicted to prescription drugs, but he'd never considered that it might affect Nancy.

He got up and paced around the living room. Nancy continued to cry silently.

"Nancy, I think you need help—we need help." He knelt beside her again. "I always wondered how you remained so calm through Kyle's death and Kelly's departure. I just thought you were really strong. Stronger than me. How blind I've been. Nancy, we've got to get you help. I couldn't bear it if anything happened to you."

"But that's what I'm trying to tell you. I've weaned

myself off of the prescriptions. I'm going to be okay—only I had no idea of how much of life I was missing." The couple embraced for a long time in the glow of Christmas lights.

"There is one thing I'd like to do," Nancy said, looking into Steve's eyes. "I want to go to church with you. And I think it's time I had a chat with Pastor McDougal. Would it be so awful if we call my brother and say we're staying home for Christmas?"

"Honey, I think it would be fine. There is going to be a houseful at your brother's. They might not even miss us if we don't come." He smiled at her and held her close.

Chapter 19

Christmas morning dawned cold and clear. The sparkly white snow made Kelly rejoice all the more. What a perfect day to celebrate the birth of the Lord Jesus, thought Kelly. Because the church celebrated on Christmas Eve, this was a day off for Kelly. He was thankful to have a few hours to himself.

He needed time to think and pray. So much had happened the last few weeks. The consequences of the terrorist attacks, now universally referred to as the "9-11" were still unfolding. His heart went out to the thousands of people facing the holiday season without their loved ones for the first time. He knew what that was like.

Nice as the day was, his heart remained under a cloud, not just for the 9-11 victims' families, but for the issues in his own life that remained unresolved. He hadn't been able to do anything about his mother's problem with prescription drugs. His concern for the youth in the church and the upcoming concern about closing Cross Church plagued him. His friend, Ted Schulte, had passed away and Jim Barnes had nearly died. The intense 24 hours he'd spent with Linda Jackson was fresh in his mind. He'd had several conversations with her since and tried to call her weekly. He missed Brianna, whom he'd only talked with once in the past several weeks. He wondered if their long-time friendship was dissolving.

Feeling as though the weight of the world was on his shoulders, Kelly dressed for the chilly morning and went to hunt up the cross-country skis someone had loaned him. Strapping them on, he began gliding slowly toward

Cottonwood Creek. With the help of his poles he skidded onto the hard surface of the frozen stream. It was so quiet that the slightest rustle of leaves was magnified. The cold sweet air seemed to help his clouded thoughts.

He'd often thought that God used nature to restore him spiritually. He remembered the momentous trip he'd taken to the mountains after Kyle had died and how much peace he'd found there. His walks along Cottonwood Creek served much the same purpose. Now he shuffled along on skis, not yet able to glide.

"Well God, I just have to ask again if I'm really the right person to be the pastor of this church," he said aloud, frightening a nearby bird that flew away with a sharp whistle. He'd been thinking of other concerns and was surprised that when he spoke out loud, his first concern was about his call to the ministry.

"Actually, I think you need someone who is wiser and better with words, someone who is more spiritual and whose personal life is settled."

Speaking out his heaviest thoughts always seemed to help. Inside his head they seemed overwhelming and true. Spoken out loud, his grumbling came into perspective. It usually brought him to the positive side of things.

He was grateful that no more big terrorist attacks had occurred and the country seemed to turn into a kinder, gentler place. The concerns about safety from terrorist attacks were far from over, but the nation was pulling together. Even though the September 11 tragedy had left the country shaken, it's true strength surfaced, and Kelly saw that as good.

He hadn't been able to do anything about his mother's problem, yet, but he had helped his father work through some grief issues.

The topic of the post-game parties came up at the last board meeting because they were a huge success. Inviting teenagers out after the game was an idea born of his desire to help the kids, which in turn was born of the dark valley he had walked as a teen. The parties seemed to be working. Now he had the board's support and a new music group for Sunday mornings.

He would miss Ted Schulte, but the older man had led a long, full life. Jim Barnes was recovering nicely, but when faced with death, he'd begun a spiritual journey likely to make the rest of his life easier.

That Linda Jackson was talking about her bitter past, was a very positive sign that she was finally coming to grips with the past.

Whether Cross Church stayed open or not was between the church board and God, he would simply trust them to make the right decision.

As for Brianna, well, he wasn't in love with her, so they were unlikely to ever marry, but their friendship would certainly survive the distance between them. Kelly had never seen so clearly what he needed to do. He needed to put to rest any thoughts of romance with Brianna.

He rounded a bend in the creek and continued shuffling along, amazed at the frozen beauty of the bare bramble branches and the dark art of rough cottonwood limbs against the sapphire sky. He stopped and took a drink from the water bottle stuffed in his oversized pocket.

Finally he began to examine all that had happened with the Golden Girl. He'd first seen her months earlier and had glimpses ever since then. Putting the bottle away, he sighed in the morning silence and even that seemed to echo. Where is she? Who is she?

"Lord, I'm confused about this woman. Am I really drawn to her or is my attention drawn by the mystery around her? This much I know--there's too much important stuff going on in my life for me to waste time thinking about this mystery. So I lay it before you. I refuse to think about her any more. I put my trust in you. If we're supposed to meet, I know you'll make it happen. Otherwise, I surrender my thoughts of her to you."

Kelly began to feel more optimistic as he prayed. He turned and began sliding toward home, thankful the McLeans had invited him to their home for Christmas dinner. He vaguely wondered who did the cooking since Jean couldn't and he wasn't certain Glen's cooking skills extended to holiday dinners. Well, no matter what they had to eat, with all those boys, it was sure to be a noisy, happy day. Maybe the boys' old maid sister does the cooking, thought Kelly, with a shrug.

After changing into a sweater and khakis, Kelly stopped at his desk and picked up the photo of Kyle and himself taken on their 16th birthday. "Merry Christmas, Kyle," he whispered. Then he ruffled Mildred's fur and went out the door, a new computer game for the McLean boys under his arm and a box of candy for the whole family.

On the way to the McLean farm he reviewed what he knew about the boys. He'd met one of them, Daniel, at the after-game parties. A senior in high school, he seemed like a nice kid and he played electronic drums. Kelly hoped Daniel would join the church band. The twins, Tim and Jim, had immediately found a special place in his heart. Kelly recalled the few times they'd been in church. They threw spit balls and teased the girls. He hated to admit it, but he was pretty sure he and Kyle had been just as naughty. The McLeans also had an older son, Adam, who farmed with his dad.

Arriving at the farm, the smell of roast turkey greeted Kelly. A wildly barking dog and the twins appeared from behind the house. They dragged him to the side door and bursting through, announced his arrival.

"Preacher's here!!"

"Hey Mom and Dad, the Preach has arrived!"

"Tim and Jim, how many times do I have to tell you to mind your manners?"

Kelly looked up to see a mass of golden curls and a spatula waving at the boys. His heart stopped as he stared at a young woman with strawberry blonde hair and the most enchanting frown.

For a long moment they stared at each other. Kelly couldn't find his voice, but his heart told him this was the girl he'd nicknamed the Golden Girl. She was blushing. Did she remember their encounter at the church?

After a long moment, she reached out her hand to him, realized it held a spatula and jerked it back.

"Hi, I'm Amber Rose. Welcome to the zoo. It wouldn't be a zoo, except we have these two wild animals that seem beyond training. Come on in." Tim and Jim scooted around her into the house.

Was this the "old maid" sister the boys talked about, he wondered? Kelly finally found his voice. "I can't say how glad I am to meet you. I guess you know I'm Pastor Kelly." They stared at each other for a few more seconds and Kelly became aware that he wore a most foolish grin and his heart thumped strangely.

"Come in the house. I just took the turkey out of the oven, so we'll be eating before long. Mom and Dad are in the living room." Amber Rose escorted Kelly through the kitchen and into the tiny living room just in time to overhear one of the twins say, "She's flirting with the preacher!" That made Amber rose turn an even deeper shade of red. Glen stood up, took each boy by the neck, and left the room for a talk.

"Adam and Daniel, I can use your help in the kitchen," Amber said, as she marched out of the room. The two older boys followed her obediently.

"I have to apologize for my sons," said Jean. "What

one doesn't think of, the other will."

"Don't worry about it. Remember, I was a twin and I got into my share of trouble."

"They like to give Amber a bad time. She's like a second mother to them, but she's still their sister. They always test her to see what they can get away with."

"Frankly, it escaped me that you had a daughter, until you mentioned her on the phone. Now I remember seeing her in church," he said as evenly as he could, "but I didn't put her in your family because, well, because she doesn't have the same color hair as the rest of you."

"Her hair is like my mother's," said Jean. Just then two repentant boys appeared in the door. "We're sorry." "We're sorry," they said, then turned to the kitchen to apologize to their sister. About that time the other guests, Sadie Jensen and Cole, arrived. Before long, dinner was served at the long kitchen table.

The meal was a blur for Kelly. He assumed they ate turkey and everything else loaded on the table, but Amber Rose sat next to him and he was much more aware of her presence than anything else. He was also hypersensitive to the beating of his own heart. Later he wondered if he'd carried on any conversation and whether he'd made any sense.

After dinner all the young people pitched in to clear the table and wash dishes, and then they brought out board games. Kelly seemed to come in last in every game, but try as he might, he couldn't make his mind think of anything but Amber Rose.

Late in the afternoon, she stretched and yawned. "I think I need a walk. Does anyone want to go with me?" Kelly prayed that no one would go, no one but him. He held his breath. Then one of the boys spoke up. "I think we should show Cole our new computer game." All the boys agreed and began trooping downstairs. The older adults had assembled in the living room. That left Amber Rose and Kelly sitting at the table alone.

Alone, Kelly thought. I'm alone with the most beautiful girl in the world! "I'd love to go for a walk," he said and she smiled shyly at him. Together they put on jackets, hats, gloves and boots. It seemed like the most intimate thing he'd ever done with a woman.

"Want to see my favorite place on the farm?" Amber asked. "It isn't fancy, but I love it." They strode toward a gate that led into the pasture. The dog, Jeep, ran circles in the pasture and occasionally took off after a rabbit. They walked through the crunchy snow toward a row of trees. On the other side of the trees was a creek. A rough wooden bench faced the creek. Behind them the sun had set, leaving a pink and purple sky.

"This is beautiful. Is this...this isn't Cottonwood Creek is it?"

Amber nodded. "I love this creek. It's so beautiful. My dream is to live by this creek forever," she said. Kelly sat still for a moment imagining the water flowing past his home and the church each day eventually flowed right past this spot as though linking them together.

"You were the girl at the church that day last summer."

"You remember that?"

"Do I! It had been a long day. I was new here and so many things had gone wrong. Then at the end of the day I walked over to the church. It was flooded with beautiful light and beautiful music." Amber blushed again.

"I've been looking for you ever since."

"You have?"

"I saw you in church once, but you left before I could talk to you. Another time I swear I saw you in a nursing home in Bismarck. I asked everyone if they knew a girl with gold curly hair that played piano, but no one knew what I was talking about. Every Sunday I'd hope to see you in the congregation. In fact, I decided if I ever saw you again, I'd stop the service and find out who you were."

Amber giggled. "So I'm a mystery woman, am I?"

"Not anymore, thank the Lord."

"I took piano lessons from Mom. She played beautifully before the multiple sclerosis took her ability away. I grew up with music filling the house and as I got older, I helped make the music.

"I work for an insurance office in Bismarck. I was probably seeing a client the day you saw me at the nursing home. And only come out here on weekends. Usually there's so much for me to do that even though I plan to go to church every Sunday, it doesn't happen. For a while I'd slip away on my way back from town and stop at the church. That was my time alone with God. That's where he seemed to fill me up, so I could continue working all week and then help out at home on weekends."

"Have you stopped there lately?"

"No. I was so embarrassed to be caught by you, that I quit."

"I'm sorry I embarrassed you. I sincerely hoped you would come back. Actually, I desperately hoped you'd come to the church."

Amber giggled again. "Why?"

"Seeing you that day, was, well I'm baring my heart here. It was one of the most extraordinary moments in my life."

"Why?"

Kelly shook his head. "I was frustrated and a little discouraged, and then all of a sudden, there you were. Beautiful, peaceful, uplifting. I was deeply touched here," he said, placing his hand over his heart.

"Do you know how I felt?" Amber asked. "As though the last private place I had was invaded. But then I learned more about who you are. You don't know me, but I've gotten to know you. I heard your sermon the Sunday when you had that fashion model with you and Linda Jackson was dying of jealousy. And Mom talks about you. I'm so glad you spend time with my parents. I realized you were a really nice guy. I mean pastor. You're a nice pastor. Oh, I can't seem to find the right words."

Kelly wanted to say, I'm a man, too, not just a pastor! But he let the thought go. "Back up a minute, while I set the record straight. That fashion model is only a friend, but if my brother was still alive, she'd probably be my sister-in-law. As for Linda Jackson, do you really think she was jealous?"

"Spitting nails, I'd say."

"No kidding. I didn't even guess that," Kelly said.

"I could just see the hot spot you were in!" she said as she turned to smile up at him. She shivered at the same time. Snowflakes like white feathers had begun to drift from the sky.

"Maybe we should go back to the house. It's getting cold."

They got up to leave and then Amber moved close to Kelly. Night had fallen, unnoticed by either of them. The scene before them might have been a Currier and Ives painting. Yellow light from the farmhouse windows in the distance cast a glow around the shabby clapboard. Outside the circle of light, the pillowy flakes fell thick.

"Shh."

Kelly cocked his head to listen to the total silence of the night. Wasn't this why he had come to North Dakota? For a place of peace and beauty where his soul could find comfort?

"Do you hear it?" Amber whispered.

Kelly strained to hear the slightest sound. Even Jeep seemed to have disappeared. If ever there were a time and place that illustrated the phrase Silent Night, Holy Night, it was here and now. A deep reverence came over Kelly, and then he heard it. Like a quilt tossed softly on a bed or flannel folding onto skin.

Amber's eyes sparkled.

He whispered, "I can hear the snow falling."

She smiled into his eyes and nodded. Then she linked her arm in his. He wanted to say so much, but his heart seemed too full. He had waited so long for this, for her.

"I hope we can be friends," she said.

"Amber Rose, I hope we become more than friends," he answered. With that he took her hand and squeezed it as they walked through the dusk, the snow falling gently around them.

Chapter 20

The happy chaos at the McLean home made the parsonage seem all the more quiet when Kelly arrived home. He turned on a lamp in the living room and spied Mildred lying on the couch. She purred contentedly and blinked at him. After shooing her off every piece of furniture in the house, he'd finally given up and placed towels wherever she seemed mostly likely to nap.

He was about to give her a good rub down when he noticed the phone message machine light was flashing. He pushed the button.

"We wish you a Merry Christmas, we wish you a Merry Christmas, we wish you a Merry Christmas and a Happy New Year!" He recognized his parents' slightly off-key singing and sudden tears stung his eyes. He'd never spent Christmas away from home before and he suddenly missed them very much. "Son, we hope you have had a really blessed Christmas. We're at home if you want to give us a call."

He immediately dialed their number and his father answered on the first ring.

"Pops!" Kelly said, reverting to the nickname he'd called his father when he was growing up. Thanks for calling. How was your Christmas?"

"Just a minute." Kelly heard scuffling sounds in the background. "There, I found a private spot so I can talk. Your mother went for a walk, but she may be back any minute and I want to talk to you privately. Kelly, we've had a remarkable holiday. You know we were going to your aunt and uncle's. Well, we cancelled our plans and had a wonderful quiet time here. We didn't even have food here, so we ordered in Chinese."

"But why didn't you go? I didn't even worry about you being alone for Christmas because I thought you had plans!"

"Well, we had plans, but God had another plan. Kelly, I've been noticing that your mother takes a lot of pills. And apparently she did too. In the past few weeks she came to see it was a problem. Apparently, she weaned herself off of them. When I came home from work yesterday, she confessed all of this to me."

Kelly slumped in his chair, awed by the unfolding news. "She told me 'Kelly has moved on, you've moved on, it's time for me to quit living in a make-believe world and start living in the present.'"

"Pops, I knew a little about the pills and they scared me. I just didn't know how to say anything. But this is good news."

"We went to the Christmas morning service! Your mother went with me and it was like we were starting all over again. Last night and today are the first time I've seen her experience real feelings for a long, long time. I've got my old girl back! What a couple days we've had. At first we mourned over the loss of Kyle. Then this morning we found real joy, together, over the Good News that a Savior has come."

Just then Kelly heard a click on the other end of the phone. "Kelly, is that you?"

"Merry Christmas, Mom!"

"Yes, it's been a wonderful Christmas—so different, but so good. But Kelly, I want to know about your Christmas. You didn't spend it alone, did you Dear?'

"Well, Pops says you had quite Christmas and so did I," Kelly began. With that he told his parents about the mysterious girl he'd seen off and on for months and how she ended up serving him Christmas dinner.

"Mom, Pops, I've never been so interested in a girl in my life."

"Not even Brianna?"

"No. Bri and I could never get a romance off the ground. I think we've both decided to give it up. But this is different. I'm going to do everything I can to get to know Amber Rose and win her heart."

"You sound a lot like me when I first met your mother. I couldn't take my eyes off of her. I wasn't at all interested in any other girl—she was the one for me and still is."

"I'll be praying for both of you," Kelly finally said, regretting he had to hang up.

"Thanks, Son. Remember how much we love you."

Chapter 21

Kelly put on his blue sweater and took it off again. He strode over to the closet and riffled through the clothes hanging there, then went back to the blue sweater. His mother had given it to him for Christmas one year, saying it matched his eyes.

"Well maybe it will make me look better," he said to Mildred, who alternately licked herself and watched him with strange fascination from her vantage point on the window ledge. He looked in the dresser mirror again, splashed on some cologne and turned around for her review.

"Well, do you think the most beautiful girl in the world will give me a chance?" he asked the ball of gray fur. "This isn't just a date, you know. This is the girl I've been searching everywhere for. She's my Golden Girl—my inspiration." Mildred yawned.

"I'll take that as a sign of approval," said Kelly as he headed out the door.

Truth be known, Kelly had been considered popular in high school and a good catch while he attended seminary, but he'd had little interest in girls. Sports and studying took his attention. Then the devastating loss of his twin brother had absorbed all of his emotions for a long time. The result was over the years he had rarely dated; but that was about to change.

His dusty blue pickup flew over the country roads toward the McLean farm. He had been there to visit a number of times and now felt foolish that he'd missed the cues that Jeanie and Glen were the parents of his Golden Girl. On the other hand, he thought, their situation seemed far removed from the darling girl with the curly golden hair who seemed to have such a luminous relationship with the Lord.

Besides, he thought as he drove, all of the other McLeans were redheads. Why would he ever think that they'd have a daughter that looked so different than the rest of the family? The focus on his visits had been on ministering to Jeanie and on the difficult financial situation the family found itself in. When Jeanie and Glen had credited their daughter with helping them, he was ashamed to admit he'd imagined her to be the old-maid type.

He had barely pulled into the yard when Amber came flying out of the house carrying her coat in her arms, although the January air was chilly. She hopped in the pickup and said, "Let's get out of here before my rascally twin brothers find out you're here!" Kelly threw the pickup in reverse and spun out of the yard.

"Was that fast enough?" he asked. Amber answered with a throaty laugh, filled with excitement.

"Hi!"

"Hi, yourself. So Tim and Jim are giving you a hard time?"

"Oh, they always do! I don't think Dad keeps them busy enough or they wouldn't be so much trouble all the time." She let out a sigh and draped her cobalt blue coat around her shoulders. "So where are we going?"

"Well if you don't mind, I heard about a restaurant over by Elmdale. It's supposed to be good and it's far enough away that maybe we won't be recognized."

"Don't want to be seen with me?"

Now it was Kelly's turn to laugh. "I can't think of anyone I'd rather be seen with. It's just that ever since I came to Cottonwood Creek, ladies have been trying to hook me up with their daughters and even though I haven't gone on one date, they've had me engaged already."

"That wouldn't have anything to do with that city girl who came to visit with your parents, would it? That looked pretty cozy to me!"

"Oh no! Not you too! Bri is a friend. Actually she was the girlfriend of my twin brother. He died when we were in high school. We've never gotten beyond a friendship over shared grief."

"I'm sorry, Kelly. I didn't know."

"Looks can be deceiving, can't they," he said with a smile. "If people actually see me with someone they will have us married off by Sunday! Hmm, actually, that wouldn't be such a bad rumor."

The restaurant sat on a paved road far from any town. As they drove up, they saw the parking lot was filled with cars and pickups.

"Must be a good place to eat," commented Kelly as he slid into a parking spot. "It isn't like it's easy to get here."

"Except it is part way between Cottonwood Creek and Harvey and Tuttle and..."

"Okay, let's say it's centrally located." He held Amber's hand on the way up the steps of the covered wood porch. The interior featured a massive native prairie stone fireplace and tables hewn out of tree trunks. Antlered trophies decorated the mantle and other spots on the walls. Kelly and Amber were lucky to get a table near the roaring fire.

"This is wonderful," Amber commented as she slid into her chair. "I love a fireplace. You know, they aren't standard in homes here. I think it's because they aren't always real heat-efficient and we need all the heat we can get this time of year. Also, when the settlers moved out here, there wasn't any wood to burn! Somehow burning cow chips in a fireplace doesn't seem the same as a nice log."

"Well, I'm glad that they put one in here. I agree—this is great. I use the fireplace in the parsonage. It seems to work okay, but I know they aren't always efficient. But hey, let's talk about something more interesting. Like you!"

"Well if that isn't a line, the weather isn't cold."

"Amber, I'm serious. I want to know everything about you from your first memory to your most recent thought."

Just then the waitress, dressed in jeans and a turtleneck, stopped by with glasses of water and menus.

"What's the special tonight?"

"Knipfla soup and prime rib of buffalo," she said, cracking her gum. "I'll be back in a minute." The limited menu included walleye, steaks, chicken and dumplings, and buffalo and beef burgers.

"Well, I haven't had buffalo since I came to North Dakota, so I think it's time. What are you having?"

"Walleye! I love fish," Amber said as she closed her menu. "In fact, I love to fish and when my life gets less complicated someday, I want to start fishing again. Nothing beats an evening catching bullheads in Cottonwood Creek."

"Bullheads?"

"Yes. I suppose there aren't any bullheads in California? When you catch one you have to watch out because they have whiskers like a catfish and they can sting you, but they taste great fried up in my special batter."

"A woman of many talents," said Kelly, leaning closer. Just then the waitress appeared to take their order. It took a while to get their food. Just enough time, in fact, to slow them down from the busy week each had just finished. The warm atmosphere cast by the roaring fire and the low sound of others talking cast them into relaxation. The mood seemed to sharpen Amber's funny bone and she began to regale Kelly with stories of growing up in Cottonwood Creek and the trouble her twin brothers always seemed to find. Kelly laughed until his sides hurt and people started looking at them. Toward the end of the meal

Kelly began telling stories on himself and Kyle, stories that he had locked away in his heart for a long time.

Finally, he became serious. "This is the first time in years I have looked back and laughed about growing up with Kyle. Until now, all I could think about was that he is gone and how much I miss him. You've helped me see the thousands of good times we had. I need to think about those more often."

Tears suddenly glistened in Amber's eyes in the firelight and she placed her hand over Kelly's, but said nothing.

"How about if we get out of here and take a drive?" Kelly asked as the check came.

"That sounds great. I can show you some of the scenic back roads in the area and maybe we can go snipe hunting."

"Snipe hunting," Kelly said as he opened the door to leave. "What's a snipe?"

"Oh, if you don't know then we really will have to do it, but not tonight. We'll wait until a warm summer night," she said with a strange smile playing around her lips. "It'll be so much more fun."

They drove for hours, as they discussed current events, the weather and how Kelly was adapting to North Dakota. When they came to a cross roads, Amber suggested they take it to Bismarck.

The night seemed magical as they slid into a booth in an all-night restaurant in north Bismarck.

"Two of your biggest, gooey desserts and two coffees," Kelly ordered when a waitress came by.

"Hmm, there goes my figure," said Amber. "I'll have one of those fudge brownies. Kelly, why don't you have the lemon pie, so I can try a bite?"

They drove back to Cottonwood Creek after midnight. A half moon hung in the sky, a willing partner with the stars in lighting the night sky.

"The colder it is, the more the stars stand out," said Amber as they took in the scene before them as they drove north. Indeed, the sky seemed like a bowl tipped over with a million stars twinkling from horizon to horizon. The snowscape met the horizon gleaming pale blue in the starlight.

After hours of talking, the couple lapsed into a congenial quiet. After a few minutes Amber said, "It came upon a midnight clear....do you think the night Christ was born that it looked like this? Have you ever thought that the shepherds were in the fields looking at the same stars we are seeing now, 2000 years later?"

"No, I've never thought about it, but the timelessness of the stars really does connect us with the first Christmas, doesn't it? I had my own starlit experience that drew me closer to Christ. It was up in the mountains after Kyle died. The stars are really clear up there, too. The Bible says that all nature points toward God and the stars really do a good job, don't they?"

Before long they neared the farm and Kelly began driving slower.

"Amber, this has been one of the best nights of my life and I don't want it to end."

"I had a great time, too. Dinner, the drive, and dessert at the all-night restaurant. But the best part was your company, Kelly."

They pulled into the yard and Jeep began barking. Amber rolled down the window and hushed him up, before lights came on in the darkened little house. The dog sat looking up at her and uttering a low, unconvinced growl, until she talked to him a little more.

"Well, I better go in before the twins wake up and come to hassle me!" Amber said. Kelly helped her out of the pickup and walked her to the door. He'd never felt so weak-kneed in his life. He wanted to grab Amber and never let her go. He wanted to kiss her as he had never kissed anyone before. Even if his face didn't give him away, his trembling hands would. Hanging on to his last shred of self control, he kissed her lightly on the mouth and backed away.

He wanted to say, "I love you!" Instead, he held her hand for a brief second more, his blue eyes now brimming with emotions he could no longer guard, and he knew she read them as she looked deep into his eyes.

A look of wonder passed over her face and then she very softly said "good night" and slipped her hand from Kelly's before disappearing through the farmhouse door.

Kelly couldn't remember driving home. As far as he was concerned, he'd flown, danced and somersaulted the eight miles to the parsonage. He was in love! If this was love, no wonder people wrote songs and poetry about it. No wonder people crossed oceans and mountains to be with someone they loved. He would do anything to be with Amber.

"Oh Father," he prayed, "Thank you for Amber! To think I have found the most wonderful girl in the world! How can I thank you enough? She is the most beautiful girl ever! And the kindest! And smartest! And sweetest! Oh, I don't deserve her in any way. What if she doesn't feel the same way about me? But she must! I'll win her heart! I'll walk barefoot in the snow to prove my love..."

Finally, Kelly realized he was home and parked in his garage. Although he had never been drunk, he was sure it must feel like this. He finally managed to get out of the pickup and into the house. He flipped on the light switch and found a sleepy-eyed Mildred waiting for him.

"Mildred!" he exclaimed, alarming the cat as he scooped her up. "I'm in love. Really in love. For the first time. It's the most wonderful thing in the whole world next to having Jesus as my Savior. Mildred, this is so great!" Mildred struggled to get away from what she considered her deranged housemate. Kelly finally put her down and did a jig around the kitchen.

"Tomorrow—no today—I'm going to call her first thing and ask her out again. We can't waste any more precious time—we've already wasted too much time when we could have been together planning our wedding. Yes, Mildred! I want to marry her!"

Just then he saw the red blinking light on his telephone answering machine. He averted his eyes. This was his supreme moment of joy. Certainly any message would be bad news about his mother, an ailing church member, a concern about an upcoming event. They could be handled tomorrow.

Kelly walked to the cupboard and scooped some cat food into Mildred's bowl. She graciously accepted it as a peace offering. He looked at the blinking light again and sighed as he pushed the button.

"Kelly, this is Bri." She sounded like she had been crying. "Everything is awful. Jontel quit and moved to Sweden to 'find his new self expression.' I hate my life here! I think I was crazy for not trying harder to find romance with you. I want to come back to the land of sunflowers. I'm coming back Kelly. I'm almost packed and I'll land in Bismarck Sunday afternoon. Please pick me up. I'll see you then."

Kelly listened to the message twice before sinking into the breakfast nook. Why now? he thought. Why right now, Bri, when I just found the love of my life? The truth is, he didn't want to be bothered. He wanted to immerse himself in his love for Amber and forget the rest of the world. He rubbed his forehead with his hands. After all the pain he'd been through, didn't he deserve happiness?

He laid his head on the table. But Brianna sounded so desperate and vulnerable. She'd been so confident the last few months, so sure of where she was going. She was a good friend—he couldn't ignore her need for help. Yet, Amber hardly knew him. How could she understand Brianna coming here?

"Oh no!" he said so loud that Mildred jumped from the rug where she'd been snoozing. "Bri thinks she can come and stay with me! She can't be that crazy to think I could let her stay here! But she might. She isn't a Christian and she doesn't understand that I can't have her here!"

The night dragged on. Kelly sifted through the issues in his mind. He could hardly believe a few short hours ago he was elated with his budding relationship with Amber and now he was in the pit of despair.

Finally he began to gain control of his thoughts. "Lord, the Bible says to take captive every thought and imagination, so that is what I am going to do. I'm going to take each one and lay it out before you and ask for your direction and intervention."

He went into the living room and lit a fire in the fireplace. He knelt beside the couch and prayed harder than he had in a long time.

Chapter 22

Kelly woke with his head on the couch and his knees on the floor. Faint morning light filtered through the living room windows and only the embers glowed in the fireplace. He stretched, yawned and sat on the couch. He must have slept a couple hours. Mildred sat perched on the coffee table and watched him.

"Ah, yes, it's breakfast time, isn't it?" The sick feeling in the pit of his stomach reminded him that he'd just had the best evening of his life topped, or maybe stopped, by untimely news. He scooped cat food into Mildred's bowl and began to pace.

"Should I call Amber and tell her the whole truth and risk losing her or call Bri and get things settled with her?" he asked Mildred. He marched to the phone and picked it up not knowing who to dial.

"Hello, is Amber there?" He rolled his eyes heavenward. Lord, my future is in your hands, he thought while he waited for her to come on the line.

"Amber your boyfriend is calling! Ha, ha, ha..."

"Hello?"

"Which one of the twins answered the phone?" he asked without introduction. After all he had already been announced.

"James the Lesser." Amber retorted.

"Amber, I had a wonderful time last night."

"So did I." Her voice softened instantly.

"Do you think we can try for another perfect evening sometime in the future—like this weekend?"

"Oh, I think that can be arranged."

"Good, consider yourself occupied by a certain pastor tonight."

"Okay, I'll see you around 7 o' clock?"

"Actually, this is really awkward, but there is something I think we need to talk about before that. Is there any way you could come over for an hour? As soon as possible?"

"There must be something really important if it can't wait until tonight..." Kelly didn't say anything. "Well, I'm on my way to town to get groceries, so I could be talked into taking the long way around..."

"Good! I'll be at the parsonage and I'll have the coffee on."

Amber arrived an hour later. It was bitter cold out and she was dressed in a green stocking cap that brought out the green of her eyes. Her nose was red from the cold.

"Oh, it's cold out there! But it's nice in here," she said looking around the kitchen and glancing into the dining and living room. Kelly poured two coffees and motioned her to take a seat at the kitchen nook. They had barely gotten seated when Mildred came strolling in, sleepy-eyed but curious about who might be visiting.

Upon seeing Amber, Mildred jumped on the bench beside her. "Oh, what a pretty kitty! I didn't know you had a cat," Amber said, stroking the appreciative fur ball.

"I don't. Mildred has me," Kelly said. He couldn't help remembering how Brianna had detested his feline roommate.

"Amber, this is really hard for me, because I don't want it to be blown out of proportion and I don't want you to be upset. If you were just any girl it wouldn't matter, but I think, I hope, our relationship is going to grow. I'm afraid if we don't talk about this you may take things the wrong way."

Amber's shoulders stiffened in anticipation of bad

news, but she didn't say anything as her finger circled the cup of coffee before her on the table. "You...you aren't secretly married are you?"

Kelly had to smile at her serious expression.

"No! But when I got home last night I had a message from an old friend—and I do mean friend—we have never dated." Kelly had been looking down, but now he looked at Amber and their eyes locked. She cocked her head and he wondered if Amber could see the fear and misery that he felt.

"It's that city girl that was here last fall."

Kelly's eyebrows raised in amazement of Amber's perceptiveness. "Yes. Brianna Davis. The history on this is that she was dating my brother when he was killed. We helped each other through the grief process and have been best of friends since then. But Amber, there has never been anything romantic between us."

"And the problem is?" Amber asked with a frown.

Kelly took a deep breath and began his explanation. "When I got home last night there was a message on my answering machine. She's on her way to Cottonwood Creek. She'll be here tomorrow. Her life is falling apart and she suddenly thinks maybe we should try to be more than friends. She thinks she can stay here!"

Amber arched an eyebrow.

"Amber, I came home last night on top of the world! And then I heard her message. Bri is, I guess, like a sister to me and I can't desert her, but I...you...I'm so worried you won't understand and that she won't understand and I...I was up most of the night trying to figure out what to do.

"I thought about fixing the problem with her before calling you again, but I don't want to spend one more day without you, so I decided to come to you first with the whole ridiculous truth."

Amber smiled. "Do you always get in these dilemmas? Is this what I can expect if we begin dating? Women begging to come live with you?"

Kelly began to relax. "Honest, Amber. This won't happen again! I promise!" he hesitated a moment, then added with a slight smile. "But the truth is, it happened before. And the last female who wanted to move in? I let her."

Amber frowned.

"She's sitting on your lap." Amber looked down at Mildred, who slept oblivious to the discussion. "Okay, let's say I believe you about all of it. What do you want me to do?"

"Mostly, I want your understanding. But, if you want to help me figure out what to do, I'd sure be obliged, ma'am."

"Well," said Amber as she got up and warmed their cups of coffee. "If you promise never to call me ma'am again, I'll help you."

Chapter 23

Conducting Sunday morning services tested his ability to put personal anxieties aside and provide spiritual food for his flock. He'd prepared his sermon early in the week and when he reviewed his notes early Sunday morning, he couldn't help but wonder if God had a sense of humor. The message seemed directed right at him.

"Our text for today is James 1: 23." He waited while the congregation paged to the passage, then read it aloud. "Consider it all joy, my brethren when you encounter various trials, knowing that the testing of your faith produces endurance." He paused for a moment before continuing. Amber sat toward the back of the room. Their eyes met and he felt something like electricity pass between them. He felt like a snowman in the sun, ready to melt into a puddle on the floor. Instead, he took a deep breath and continued.

"When you're in the middle of a trial, you may think, 'You've got to be kidding!' How can I possibly find joy in the middle of a trial? Students, when there is an unexpected test in school, does that make you want to do a happy dance? How about you farmers, as you watch a hail storm sweep over your healthy, vibrant crops? What about when you get a difficult diagnosis from your doctor? How easy is it to find joy in those moments?"

Across the congregation, a few heads nodded in agreement, but for the most part people sat expressionless. Kelly had learned that his congregation generally didn't show much emotion, but that didn't mean he wasn't getting through to them. He pushed on.

"So the question is, how do you find joy in the midst of a trial? How do you? I'm so grateful that God provides a road map for us, directions, a recipe, for living in that realm where you can experience joy in the middle of a trial.

"The answer may be found in the next book of the Bible. James 5: 7 states, 'Cast all your cares upon him, for he cares for you.'

"Yes, he cares for us, just like a mother cares for her baby. And just like a mother has the power to help a helpless baby, God has the power to help us. So we can cast our cares upon him.

"But wait—there's more. The scripture preceding this one gives us a hint at how to find that comfort and joy in God. James 5: 6 states that we must humble ourselves under the mighty hand of God. In other words, the way to find joy and peace no matter what the circumstance is to live in a continual relationship with God. That way, when those trials come to us, we won't have to go through the whole process of being reacquainted.

"Have you ever had someone contact you after a long period of time, only to find out they just wanted something from you?"

Kelly paused here, shocked by a new thought—Brianna had not kept in touch with him for the last several months, but now she suddenly needed his help and expected him to pick up the relationship on her terms. He suddenly felt like he was preaching a sermon to himself.

He lost his train of thought and looked down at his notes for a moment.

"Well, God doesn't like it either when we only look him up when we need him. That's why we must keep our relationship with God fresh every day. The way to know joy in a trial is by never turning off the connection we have with our savior, Jesus Christ. He is our path to God and the source of our spiritual power in every trial."

His eyes sought Amber's and he could see her nodding, bright emotion on her face. He thought she might understand what he'd just figured out.

The service closed with an old song. "Turn your eyes upon Jesus, look full in his wonderful face and the things of earth will grow strangely dim in the light of his glory and grace."

Kelly rushed back to the parsonage as soon as he could after the service. He hadn't heard from Brianna since receiving the phone message saying she was giving up on her life in San Francisco and moving to North Dakota. She'd ended the phone call by asking him to pick her up in Bismarck late Sunday afternoon. He'd tried calling her home phone and her cell phone numerous times, without reaching her.

To his relief, his answering machine was blinking. He listened to the call from Brianna explaining that she'd gotten as far as Denver, when all flights were canceled due to a snowstorm. She asked him to call her cell phone as soon as possible.

He walked around the living room, praying for guidance, then picked up the phone and dialed Brianna's number.

"Kelly? I'm glad to hear from you. It's snowing and blowing outside. All the flights are cancelled. There are a million people here. I carved out a spot for myself on the floor. This is crazy. Do you have snow in North Dakota?"

"Door to door—about two feet deep."

"How can you stand it?"

"Well I kind of looked forward to it. Did you know I got caught in a blizzard already? Had to stay overnight at a café..."

"Kelly," Brianna cut off his story. "I thought I wanted to move out there, but I'm not prepared for that. I don't have any winter clothes. I'm a California girl!"

"We can find some clothes for you and get you outfitted right away. I'll even buy you a snowmobile suit and snow boots."

"Yew. Kelly, I don't know what to do. This career thing really blew up in my face. The truth is I can take over the business in San Francisco, but I'm so disillusioned. I thought maybe coming out there was the right thing to do. You know those sunflowers ended up being the only bright thing in my work here!"

"Bri, you should come here," Kelly said firmly. "I talked it over with Amber Rose and she agrees you should come out here and start over." He loved the way her name rolled off his tongue. Amber Rose. Amber Rose.

"Who is Amber Rose?"

"Well, that's a little hard to explain...we've only been on one date, but somehow..."

"You mean you have a girlfriend?"

"Ah, well, yes it looks like it."

"So there's no hope for me."

"That's not true. We talked it over. We think you should come out. Amber actually lives in Bismarck and her roommate is moving away, so you could share an apartment with her while you look for work."

"You want me to share an apartment with your new girlfriend an hour's drive from you."

"Yes."

"That's a lot to think about."

"Brianna?"

"Yes?"

"You've been my best friend for a long time and you'll always have a place in my heart. This is not the end of things—this is the beginning. If I've learned anything since Kyle died, it's that there is a God and he gives second chances. When we think there is only Plan A and Plan B, he has Plan C prepared and waiting for us.

"Now you can come to Bismarck or you can go back to California. But before you make a big decision about your next step, will you promise me you will ask God for direction?"

After a long pause, Brianna finally spoke. "It took me a long time to come to the end of myself didn't it? It took a long time and now I'm stuck in a snowstorm all alone in a strange city. I turn to you and you point me to God. Just like Kyle did."

"My question is, Bri, are you there yet? You've seen Kyle's life and my life change because we found the mercy of God. What are you waiting for?"

"I don't know. I truly don't know. Listen, I probably won't be able to fly anywhere before tomorrow. Let me think about this...and pray about it. I'll call you tonight."

After he hung up, Kelly felt Mildred wrap around his legs. He swept her up and scratched her behind the ears until she purred. Then he dropped her in a chair and reached for the phone again.

"Hello. Is Amber Rose there?"

"Hey Amber, it's your boyfriend, the Preach!"

Kelly leaned against the wall and laughed out loud as he waited for Amber to come on the line. He'd truly found joy in the midst of this trial.

Epilogue

Ezekiel 47 is an allegory of a life-giving river that flows from the throne of God giving the reader an inspired vision of God's provision. The river flows wide and free, teeming with life and refreshing all it touches, bringing hope and a promise of an abundant future.

Water played an important part in Jesus' ministry on earth as recorded in the New Testament. He recruited fishermen to be his disciples. He stilled a storm that threatened to swamp the boat in which he sailed. He urged his followers to give a cup of water to those who are thirsty.

Jesus was a very earthy, practical man, who was familiar with Ezekiel's river of God. He knew if we walk in friendship with God, His living water will flow to us and through us. Jesus' deep relationship with God gave him extraordinary power; power he promised to leave with his followers; power we can still receive today when we have friendship with him.

Sometimes that water comes in the form of a river, sometimes it comes in a cup and sometimes it flows to us in a small wandering body of water such as Cottonwood Creek.

In a marshy pasture off County Road 10 somewhere in central North Dakota, a spring bubbles to the soggy surface, flooding the low land and creating a gathering place for wildlife. Families of geese return to the marsh each spring to raise flocks of goslings; muskrats scurry through the tall reedy grass; and turtles warm themselves on sun-drenched rocks jutting above the prairie pothole.

The water seems to gather at the south end of the depression, as though waiting to make a journey, then spills into a shallow ravine, spreading wide across its breadth.

Then the stream flows through a culvert under the road and trickles along the ditch for a quarter of a mile. Veering to the southeast, the stream picks up speed as it tumbles down a hill and into another gully that curves to the west and then south again before it reaches the section line. A mile has passed, though Cottonwood Creek has twisted two. A bridge is required at this point. It's a handsome little concrete bridge built by the CCC boys back in the 1930s. That it is sturdy so many decades later is a testament to the skill of those hardy workers.

The stream now has banks. It widens and narrows with no thought of conformity. Along its banks grow heavy cottonwood trees, their wide branches sprawling, now over the creek and now over the prairie grass waving in the breeze. Wide green leaves shade cattle and horses, fishermen and small boys who explore the creek running through pasture lands. In the autumn, cottonwood leaves struggle through a month of frosty nights before the life freezes from them. Floating to the ground, the breeze whips them up and carries them to their winter nesting place, where decaying under the snow they nourish the earth as it prepares for the spring renewal.

Within the banks of the creek is a world teeming with life. Bullheads and sunfish laze in the clear water, perch wiggle through the cool darkness in constant search of food. Crawdads and snails feed on the richness of the algae. In some places Cottonwood Creek returns to its marshy roots, the water serving as a giant vase for cattails and other reedy water plants. A short while later it may be narrow and deep enough for a two-man boat.

It flows under the footbridge that links Cottonwood Church on the east with the parsonage on the west. Then it generously widens enough for summer swimming and winter skating parties. In the shade of its trees, church picnics and summer Bible school classes have enriched the lives of the congregation for generations. And at least one young pastor embraced his true love on the little arched wooden foot bridge and proposed a lifetime together.

Cottonwood Creek flows onward, twisting south, flowing right past the McLean farm and turning west until it resolutely pours itself into the Missouri River, abandoning its life-giving mission to the greater.

In the spring of 2002, Amber Rose McLean and Kelly Jorgenson stood near the little footbridge on Cottonwood Creek, half way between the church and the parsonage, and pledged to spend their lives together. The creek babbled happily in the background. Lavender lilacs spilled from giant baskets filling the air with their heavenly scent. In the background, the ladies of the church had set tables in the church yard with a tall white-frosted wedding cake in a special spot. The Pastor McDougal performed the ceremony while their families and friends looked on.

Kelly glanced at his father, whom he'd chosen as his best man and then at his mother, who smiled and nodded at him from the front row. Glen McLean stood with his hands on his wife's wheelchair, thankful that Jeanie was able to attend. He saw, too, that his four red-headed new brothers-in-law stood together, the older ones keeping the wily younger boys in check. Beyond the family, were many friends he'd come to know in the past year, and then there was Brianna Davis. He still couldn't believe Amber had asked Brianna to be her bridesmaid. He had to wonder at the amazing turns of events since that winter day when a snowstorm in Denver had changed Brianna's life forever.

Amber Rose stood facing him, her angelic face and

golden hair glowing in the spring sunshine. He closed his eyes a moment and opened them again, just to make sure she really stood there in a simple, long white gown. She held a bouquet of lilies of the valley. Kelly took a deep breath to calm himself, then looked again at the creek and realized it had become his favorite spot in the world and he was marrying the most wonderful woman in the world right on its banks.

The clear voice of a young tenor began singing The Lord's Prayer and a hush fell over the people gathered there. Kelly reached for Amber Rose's hand, sure that the God who had brought them together would take them the rest of the way.

And so it is for some, that the river of God can be found in a creek, rich in God-inspired life and full symbolism of his unending mercy and intimate care of our lives.

~END~

Discussion Questions

1. Kelly feels "called" to ministry in North Dakota, but he also longs to put his past behind him. Which feeling to you think is stronger?

2. Kelly is enthusiastically welcomed when he arrives at Cottonwood Church. Is this kind of neighborliness unique to rural areas? Have you participated in or been the recipient of a warm welcome?

3. The relationship Kelly has with Brianna Davis is complex. Do you think it's possible for a man and woman to have a close relationship without becoming romantic?

4. Why do you think Linda Jackson and Kelly disliked each other right away? Why do you think the trauma they experienced as teens led them down different paths?

5. Amber Rose McLean is willing to sacrifice almost anything to help her family. What do you think is the source of her character and strength?

6. What do you think is the significance of the Jorgenson party being at the International Peace Gardens on 9-11?

7. Kelly is upset to hear about the teens' drinking parties. Do you think it's all right for teens to drink? What alternatives would you propose?

8. Why do you think it takes some people a long time to come to grips with tragedy, yet others are able to move on in spite of their pain?

9. Kelly pursues the elusive Amber Rose McLean, but finally surrenders his hope of finding her. Have you ever given up on a dream, only to have it come true?

10. Were you surprised that Kelly marries Amber Rose rather than Brianna?

About the Author

Gayle Larson Schuck holds a bachelor's degree in communications. She worked in the fields of public information, public relations and development for 28 years. She is a Bible study teacher and chairs the missions committee at her church. Gayle enjoys sharing outdoor adventures with her husband, children and grandchildren.

49235785R00117

Made in the USA
Middletown, DE
10 October 2017